"I've got to leave here, Leith."

"Was I wrong to think what I did? That if I reached out to touch you . . ."

"Leith!" she cried out in protest.

"You do want me," he breathed, then dazed her beyond any reply by pouring a passionate rain of kisses over her hair. "The why or how of it doesn't matter. We were meant to come together, Suzanne."

"You mustn't . . ."

"No." His lips grazed over hers, leaving the words in her mind stillborn. "Don't say anything," he whispered, his breath as warmly seductive as his mouth. "Feel it with me. Let me show you."

EMMA DARCY nearly became an actress until her fiancé declared he preferred to attend the theater *with* her. She became a wife and mother. Later, she took up oil painting—unsuccessfully, she remarks. Then she tried architecture, designing the family home in New South Wales. Next came romance writing—"the hardest and most challenging of all the activities," she confesses.

EMMA DARCY

The Shining of Love

Harlequin Books

TORONTO • NEW YORK • LONDON
AMSTERDAM • PARIS • SYDNEY • HAMBURG
STOCKHOLM • ATHENS • TOKYO • MILAN
MADRID • WARSAW • BUDAPEST • AUCKLAND

ISBN 0-373-11632-2

THE SHINING OF LOVE

A Note from the Author

Fourteen of the world's unwanted children were gathered into the James family from different countries, and at different ages, some of them suffering from experiences they had been subjected to before being rescued by the two wonderful people who adopted them and turned their lives around.

Tiffany had the easiest path into the family. She had no memory of any other life. Although not Fijian, she had been left on the doorstep of a church in Suva, a newborn baby whose mother could not be found or identified. This never troubled Tiffany. To her mind, she belonged to the greatest family in the world and wanted no other. Every day was an adventure, and life was to be seized and made beautiful. Determined to set up the best possible future for her crippled brother, Tiffany plunged into organising a tourist development on the Gold Coast of Queensland, and it was her zest and optimism for this project that brought her to the man she was to love in the story *Ride the Storm*, HP#1401.

Rebel was seven years old when she was adopted into the James family. Her English mother had been one of the war orphans shipped to Australia in 1944. Whoever her father was, he was long gone before Rebel was born, and when she was five years old, her mother died and she was fostered out to people who exploited such children. She continually ran away and was labelled as an uncontrollable child by the welfare people. Found and rescued by the James family, she grew into a woman who could take on the world in her own inimitable style, and in the book *Dark Heritage,* HP#1511, she took on the Earl of Stanthorpe over his treatment of a child. This story is set in England, at Davenport Hall, where Rebel's mother had been briefly housed before being shipped to Australia. Childhood memories of her mother's stories took Rebel there. Unbeknownst to her, her mother's parents had traced their lost daughter to the same place. In the course of her battle to win the hearts of both the earl and the child, Davenport Hall became the meeting ground for Rebel and her maternal grandparents to find each other.

Suzanne was three years old when she was adopted into the James family. She was orphaned by the death of her father in a rodeo event at the Calgary Stampede in Canada. No-one came forward to claim her. She never knew what had happened to her mother. Suzanne's story reflects the person she has become. It begins in the Australian outback where... But you can read all about it in this book, *The Shining of Love.*

CHAPTER ONE

THE LOST CHILD couldn't survive in this searing heat. Not in the unforgiving outback. Not without water. Not without someone to find protection for her. The search was almost certainly futile. It was far too late for Amy Bergen to be found. Not alive, anyway.

Where she had wandered, or what had taken her away from the scene of her parents' tragic death probably would never be known. It was a depressing thought to Suzanne, and her heart went out to the little girl's family who had enough grief to carry without the added pain of never knowing the fate of a much loved child.

There was a finality about death that could be accepted. Eventually. But lost.... Suzanne knew the nagging torment of endless wondering all too well.

Her father had died when she was three years old. She knew that for a fact. The wonderful couple who had subsequently adopted her had been in Calgary for the rodeo when it happened, and they had told her the story many times. The Canadian officials had been unable to trace any family for her, so Suzanne didn't know, and had no chance of ever knowing, what had happened to her mother.

Sometimes she believed her mother had to be dead, because she couldn't accept a mother who deserted her daughter and never once looked back to find out how she fared. Yet if she was alive, where was she? What kind of life had she led? What kind of life was she living now?

It was the not knowing that hurt the longest. It never went away. It could be submerged for days or weeks or months, but it always crept out again in lonely moments. Or when something like this happened.

Suzanne ruefully thought she could do with a bit of cool Canada right now. Central Australia would have to be the starkest contrast to the country on the top half of the North American continent, but she had chosen to make her life here and she was content with her choice.

She drove through the township of Alice Springs with all the car windows open. It didn't help much to lessen the heat in the car, but there was no point in switching on the air-conditioning while the interior was still like an oven. She used a towel on the steering wheel to prevent her hands from burning, and despite the protective seat cover, she felt as though she was sitting in a sauna.

Fortunately it was no great distance from the community services complex, where she held a morning clinic for the aboriginal women and their children, to the medical centre that claimed the rest of her working hours. Today was not the kind of day that stirred people to any unnecessary activity and there was little traffic in the streets. Five more minutes and she would be out of this oppressive heat and inside her blissfully cool office.

The thick mass of her wavy black hair was sticking to her neck by the time she alighted from her car. She pushed it up with her arm, wishing she had tied it into a high ponytail. There was not the slightest waft of a breeze. She let it drop to her shoulders again as she walked along the path from the car park to the main entrance of the medical centre.

Out of the corner of her eye, she noticed a man stepping out of a taxi, but Suzanne didn't really look at him. Her mind was savouring the thought of a long icy drink.

Their paths met under the portico. The man paused to let her precede him. She automatically flashed him a commiserating smile. A comment about the heat was on the tip of her tongue when recognition froze it there. Something more than recognition halted her feet.

She had the oddest sense of deja vu as their eyes met. Her mind reasoned that of course she had seen him before. The media coverage on the family tragedy that had brought this man to Alice Springs was still intense, and Suzanne had watched him being interviewed on television several times.

Nevertheless, that did not explain such an eerie impact at meeting him in person, almost as though they had always been meant to meet, to connect in some important way.

He was staring into her darkly lashed violet eyes, an intense, searching look, as though he also felt some inexplicable inner jolt.

Leith Carew.

Suzanne turned his name over in her mind, reviewing what she knew of him. He was the eldest son of the legendary Carew family of the Barossa Valley, winemakers for five generations, owning and adding to a vineyard that was famous not only in South Australia, but around the wine-drinking nations in the world. Leith Carew was the business manager, running the head office in the capital city of Adelaide.

It was his sister who had died out in the desert, his sister, Ilana, and her husband, Hans Bergen, the master vintner. The lost child was their two-year-old daughter, the first and only child of the sixth generation. Leith Carew was unmarried, and his twin half-brothers were in their early teens.

Suzanne had thought him impressive on television, a man in command of himself and those around him, using the media to get across the message he wanted and deftly turning away any attempt to sensationalise his role as the representative and driving force of the Carew family.

He was quite strikingly handsome, the combination of dark blond hair and green eyes lending an unusual attraction to what was essentially a hard face. His smoothly tanned skin seemed to be stretched tightly over prominent cheekbones and the angular cut of his jawline. There were few lines to indicate age, but the maturity of his features and the position of responsibility he held placed him in his early to mid-thirties. A slight bump on his strong nose suggested a break he hadn't bothered to have straightened out. Probably playing football in younger days, Suzanne thought, considering his well above average height and muscular physique.

The light tropical suit he wore was as classy as the rest of him, quality fabric, restrained style. He didn't need ostentation to stand out from a crowd. He had the air of being master of any hand he wanted to play.

Suzanne sensed he had been tipped slightly off balance in the last few moments. As she was. By some odd link between them.

Psychic?

Sexual?

As Suzanne hastily rejected this last thought she saw a sceptical gleam emerge in the piercing green eyes, mocking either her or himself. It evoked a wave of prickling heat that owed nothing to the high temperature of the day. She was suddenly and embarrassingly conscious of acting like a morbid gawker in the face of a man who had been forced into the public limelight by tragic circumstances.

"Can I help you, Mr. Carew?" she asked in a sympathetic rush.

His grimace expressed a weary resignation at her ready identification of him. His gaze flicked to her nurse's uniform, making another assessment of her before he replied.

"You work here?"

"Yes. Most of the time."

"It's a fine service you people give to the outback community," he remarked appreciatively.

Suzanne smiled. The medical centre was attached to the Royal Flying Doctor Base that served the remote outback cattle stations and the aboriginal settlements of inland Australia. It was a unique medical service that always impressed visitors.

"Someone has to do it," she said with a touch of pride in what was achieved here, despite the difficulties that had to be overcome.

"Few would volunteer."

"It depends on what kind of life you want."

"Is it the life you want?" he asked curiously.

Suzanne considered for a moment before answering the question seriously. "It has more personal rewards than working in a big city hospital."

"What about your private life?"

"It's all I want."

"Is it?" The soft challenge in his voice was reinforced by a suggestive simmer in his eyes.

Jolted by the overt sexual interest he was showing, Suzanne instantly retreated into formality. "Is
there any way I can help you, Mr. Carew?"

The reminder of his business at the medical centre drew a grim mask over his expression. "I'm here
to see a Dr. Forbes. Could you show me where to
go?"

"I'll take you straight to him," Suzanne offered, unnerved at finding herself uncomfortably
conscious of being a woman in the presence of this
man.

He exuded a powerful masculinity that he was at
ease with, and was apparently well aware of its effect. "Thank you," he said with a knowing look
that increased Suzanne's disquiet.

He was used to women going out of their way for
him, she thought with another hot feeling of mortification. She turned quickly, welcoming the cool
air of the lobby as the entrance doors slid open automatically. She half wished she had only offered
directions to Brendan's office, but it was petty to let
Leith Carew's attraction sway her from a more
sympathetic course.

It was bad enough that he had to suffer being in
the public eye at a time of private grief. His mission here this morning certainly had nothing to do
with capitalising on his good looks. Nevertheless,
Suzanne felt a distinct unease as she led the way
down the corridor to the administration offices.

Her initial response to Leith Carew should have been one of instinctive compassion. Why had a more personal feeling blocked that out? Even now she was far more tuned to the vitality of the man walking beside her than to the dreadful sense of loss that must be eating at him. It put Suzanne completely out of sorts with herself.

Her rap on the chief medical officer's door was unnecessarily sharp. With an assurance that no-one at the centre would question, Suzanne did not wait for an answer. She opened the door and poked her head around it. Brendan lifted his attention from the stack of paperwork on his desk and shot her a warm welcoming smile.

It should have made her feel happy and secure. This was the man she loved for a host of good reasons. But quite unreasonably Suzanne was more aware of the man waiting behind her in the corridor, and somehow that awareness stopped her from returning Brendan's smile.

"I've brought Mr. Leith Carew to see you," she said bluntly.

Brendan was instantly all business, the smile wiped from his face as he rose from his chair to come and greet the visitor. Suzanne opened the door wide and ushered in the man who was still profoundly disturbing her.

"Mr. Carew." Brendan offered his hand in sympathetic respect.

"Dr. Forbes."

Suzanne watched them size each other up as they went through the formalities of establishing a professional rapport. They were approximately the same age, but Leith Carew was the taller, bigger man, his wider and more worldly experience of life somehow dominating this encounter.

Suzanne felt a stab of disloyalty at the comparison. Leith Carew's harder edge did not diminish Brendan's quiet assurance. Besides, it was the heart of a man that mattered more than anything else. There were always kindness and compassion in Brendan's soft brown eyes, and while he might not be so handsome as to turn women's heads, he had the type of face that inspired trust and confidence.

Brendan Forbes was a good man with a big heart. As big as Zachary Lee's. And any man who measured up to her eldest adopted brother's heart was number one with Suzanne.

His eyes flashed a message that she understood only too well as he spoke to her. "Would you tell reception to hold over all calls to me while I'm with Mr. Carew, Suzanne?"

Painful business, best handled without interruption. She nodded and started to withdraw, pulling the door shut after her.

"Suzanne..."

Leith Carew spoke her name as though rolling his tongue around it, tasting it, savouring it. It sent a shiver down her spine. She instinctively squared her shoulders, fighting off his unwelcome effect on her.

Courtesy demanded she acknowledge him one last time. She looked, meeting a green-eyed gaze that held a determined promise he would find her again at a more opportune time.

"Thank you," he said.

She bit down on the automatic response, "You're welcome." He wasn't welcome. He had twisted the indefinable link that had leapt between them into something totally wrong and unacceptable.

She gave a brief nod to satisfy Brendan's sensitivity to the situation, then firmly shut the door, leaving the two men to get on with what had to be done.

The post-mortem reports, most likely, Suzanne thought, wincing over the horror of hearing the grim results of what could have been avoided if only Ilana and Hans Bergen had understood the terrain they had travelled.

Tourist brochures billed the Australian outback as the last frontier, an adventure into a primitive timeless landscape that defied the encroachment of civilisation. The dangers involved in setting out without an experienced guide were well publicised, but every year there were people who believed they knew enough and were properly prepared to meet and beat any possible mishap on their own. And every year the outback took its toll of them.

Ilana and Hans Bergen had decided to travel the Gunbarrel Highway, so named because the track had been bulldozed in a dead straight line across the desert by a geological survey team. It was not maintained and was barely negotiable by the hardiest four-wheel-drive vehicle. What had drawn the Bergens off that track no-one knew. Perhaps the mirage of a lake. The area where they were eventually found was nicknamed the Dunes of Illusion.

The outcome was easy enough to piece together afterwards. They had driven over high spinifex, which had been caught up and compressed under the metal guards of their Land Rover. Since spinifex was full of combustible gum, it ignited against the hot exhaust.

The couple had obviously panicked and tried to put the fire out with their water supply. They were left with little or no water and an undriveable vehicle. Their fate was inevitable. In the Gibson Desert temperatures could reach fifty degrees Celsius at midday.

Suzanne delivered Brendan's message to the receptionist and retreated to her own office. She automatically filed cards on the aboriginal families she had seen that morning. Although there was nothing of a serious nature to report, she was meticulous about keeping records. One never knew what might be important some day.

It was the lack of any records on her father that had made tracing any family impossible. Not that it really mattered now, Suzanne told herself. After all, she had been brought up in the greatest family in the world, fourteen lost children taken in by the kindest and most loving parents, who taught them how to blend together and support each other. She was proud to be one of the James family.

They had all been encouraged to be achievers in their own individual ways, and Suzanne had found a very real fulfilment in her nursing career. Brendan was the perfect partner for her. In that sense, Leith Carew had nothing to offer her, and she had nothing to offer him.

She frowned over his reaction to her. Why would such a man even bother to show an interest, let alone feel one? It wasn't as though she was strikingly attractive.

She had a slim, trim figure nicely proportioned to her average height, but it was hardly spectacular. She was lucky with the natural wave of her hair, and her eyes were certainly attractive in shape and colour. She wished her nose wasn't tip tilted, since it always caught the sun if she didn't wear a hat, and she would have preferred not to have a dimple in her chin. But she counted herself passably pretty. More than passably compared to most of the young women who populated Alice Springs.

She had no doubt Leith Carew could choose from the cream of society in more than this continent, and in such a wide field of beautifully polished and sophisticated women, Suzanne felt sure she would be quite ordinary.

Perhaps, for him, she had simply been an on-the-spot diversion from burdens that were weighing too heavily on him. She wished he hadn't reacted like that. It had made her feel wrong instead of . . .

Instead of what?

Suzanne shook her head in vexation. Forget it, she sternly told herself. It couldn't have been important. And Leith Carew would soon go back to his own world, which was a long, long way from hers.

She immersed herself in paperwork, not looking up from her desk until a knock came on her door. Brendan, she thought, but it was Leith Carew who stepped into her office.

Again Suzanne was gripped by a sense of something meaningful that went beyond any logical reasoning. It ran through her mind that this man had a part to play in her life or she had a part to play in his. Improbable as that was, the strange feeling could not be easily dismissed.

He closed the door behind him and stood in front of it for several moments, his eyes probing hers for answers he wanted or needed. There was a rigidity about his body that suggested he was holding a tight control over himself. He looked sick.

"I wondered—" he started forward as he spoke "—if you were free this evening. I'd like to have your company."

"I'm sorry, Mr. Carew. I'm not free," Suzanne answered softly, realising the medical reports Brendan would have read to him must have conjured up images that would have been harrowing.

He picked up the solid glass paperweight from her desk, rolled it around in his hand, then gripped it hard as though he needed to hold onto something solid. His gaze slowly lifted to hers again, a compelling intensity in the dark green depths.

"I know we've barely met, but I feel you're someone I can talk to. Be with. Won't you give me your company for one evening? Help me forget . . . other things . . . for a while? There's nothing for you to be wary of—" he winced "—unless being seen with me is too distasteful."

"No, it's not that," Suzanne assured him gently. He was hurting badly, but she couldn't give him the solace he was looking for. "I'm simply not free to be with you, Mr. Carew."

He frowned. "Couldn't you cancel whatever arrangements you've made? I'm only asking . . ."

"No. I'm sorry, but no," Suzanne said firmly.

His face tightened. His mouth compressed in frustration with her outright rejection. The appeal in his eyes hardened to an arrogance that challenged her decision. "Tell me what arrangements you've made and I'll speak to the person or persons concerned."

He was not used to being refused. Suzanne offered him an ironic little smile. "You misunderstand me, Mr. Carew. I am not free. I have a husband. And you've just been speaking to him."

He stared at her with a look of stunned disbelief. "You're married . . ."

"To Dr. Forbes," Suzanne finished for him with quiet dignity.

Leith Carew visibly shuddered. His gaze dropped to the paperweight in his hand. His fingers tightened around it, and from the way his knuckles gleamed white Suzanne thought he would have crushed the glass to powder if it was possible.

His tension stirred the same unease he had evoked earlier. Suzanne's sympathy for him was stretched thin. Although his meeting with Brendan could never have pleasant associations for Leith Carew, surely he realised that was not Brendan's fault. She resented the look of repugnance on his face.

"How long have you been married?" he suddenly shot at her.

Surprised by the question, she answered automatically. "Almost three years."

"And the magic hasn't worn off yet?"

The mockery in his voice suggested a soul-deep cynicism, and there was a flare of savagery in the eyes that slashed at hers. Suzanne recoiled both mentally and emotionally from all he was projecting at her, yet even as a cutting retort leapt to her tongue, she bit down on it. He was reacting like a wounded animal. She had disappointed him. It would be wrong to hit back at him for lashing out at her.

"Our marriage doesn't depend on magic, Mr. Carew," she said calmly, her eyes holding his with steady, heartfelt conviction. "It's based on commitment to each other."

"Till death do you part?"

"Yes. That's how it is for Brendan and me."

He challenged that contention for several angry moments before the feral glitter in his green eyes faded into a bleak sadness. He looked at the paperweight, then slowly replaced it on her desk.

"That's how it was for Ilana and Hans," he said with bitter irony.

"I'm sorry," Suzanne murmured, compassion spearing through the turbulence he had stirred.

He gave her a twisted smile. "Forgive me for trespassing. And thank you for your time."

He turned and walked to the door. Suzanne was riven by the sense of unfinished business between them, yet she knew she couldn't answer the need that he had opened to her.

"Goodbye, Mr. Carew," she said softly, hoping he would find solace for his pain with someone else.

"No. Not goodbye," he rasped, then looked at her, his eyes burning with a conviction that defied barriers. "We'll meet again, Suzanne Forbes. The timing isn't right, here and now, but the day and the hour will come when it is."

His words seemed to thump into her heart. He had felt it, too, she thought dazedly.

"*Au revoir,* Suzanne," he said with very deliberate emphasis.

He closed the door on this encounter and walked out of her life. Until their paths crossed at another time and place. But when? And why? Suzanne wondered. Her hand reached out and picked up the solid glass paperweight. His fingers had dulled its natural gleam. It felt cold. She shivered and thrust it away from her.

I love Brendan, she thought fiercely. *I'll love him all my life. Leith Carew can't change that. Nothing ever will.*

A surge of totally irrational feeling made her snatch up the paperweight again and drop it into the bottom drawer of her desk. Out of sight.

CHAPTER TWO

THE PROBLEM of Leith Carew did not go away.
Suzanne wished she had not met him. The memory of his powerful presence and personality kept
sliding between her and Brendan, intruding on the
natural intimacy they had built up between them.

Normally she talked to Brendan about everything of interest that happened at the clinic or the
centre, but something held her back from relating
the details of Leith Carew's private visit to her. She
even affected a disinterest in Brendan's comments
on the man, quickly turning the subject aside in favour of a less disturbing topic of conversation.

Rightly or wrongly, she felt Leith Carew was
somehow a threat to the happiness of her marriage. He had left her with a sense of inevitability
that could not be denied or repressed. The day and
the hour would come when they would meet again.
Suzanne was afraid of what it might mean to her,
so she did her best to deny him any space in her life.

Three days after his visit to the medical centre,
Leith Carew was on the evening news. His strong
face leapt out at her from the television set, mak-

ing her heart skip a beat. She could no longer view him as a two-dimensional person.

"I'll start putting on dinner," she said, leaving Brendan to watch the news alone while she raced off to the kitchen to busy herself with their evening meal.

He followed a few minutes later. "They've called off the search for Amy Bergen," he said with a grimace that expressed his repugnance for any unnecessary loss of life.

"Why?" Suzanne cried in dismay. Her mind told her there had been no hope of survival for the little girl, yet as long as she wasn't found, hope persisted anyway.

"They've recovered a piece of her clothing."

"Not the child?"

Brendan shook his head. "Only the clothing. But it was close to a dingo's lair."

"Oh, God!" It instantly recalled the Azaria Chamberlain case, when a nine-week-old baby had been taken by a dingo from the camping site at Ayers Rock. "But Amy Bergen was two years old," Suzanne protested. "Surely..."

"The police think it's conclusive."

"No other trace of her?"

"Apparently not. It's hardly to be expected after this length of time, Suzanne," he added softly.

Her shoulders slumped. "No. I suppose not."

"Leith Carew isn't prepared to accept it. Understandable enough."

"Yes," she bit out, concentrating fiercely on tearing up lettuce leaves. The Leith Carews of this world weren't good at accepting anything they didn't like. But he had to, she thought grimly, when he had no other choice.

Whether that triggered the next thought that came into her mind, Suzanne did not stop to consider. She turned impulsively to Brendan and the words spilled from her lips. "I think it's time we started a family. Are you ready to be a father, Brendan?"

The change in his expression lifted Suzanne's heart. His grin was a glorious beam of delight and his eyes sparkled with happiness. "More than ready if you are, my darling," he said as he swept her into his arms.

There followed a night of sweet plans and intense loving that comprehensively wiped Leith Carew from Suzanne's mind.

The idea of having a baby was still a warm glow inside her the next morning as she checked the progress of the babies brought to the clinic by their proud mothers. Suzanne had always loved this part of her work at the community services complex.

It had taken a while for the aboriginal people to accept her as someone who could give helpful advice on health problems. It had probably been easier for her than for any other nurse, because both she and Tom James had been adopted into the same family, and although there was no blood link between them, she was accorded the status of his sister.

They trusted Tom. It was he who had persuaded the government to build this facility, and he had been the driving force behind establishing the progressive programs that not only focussed on their present and future welfare, but kept their ancient culture a positive and proud force in their lives.

Here their art and folklore were practised and preserved for future generations. Community councils were held to settle disputes and set goals that concentrated on self-sufficiency rather than a reliance on government funds. In former years there had been much misunderstanding about the social system of the indigenous Australians but it was given more respect now, thanks to people like Tom, who formed a bridge between the old world and the new.

Since she had married Brendan, Tom had been teasing Suzanne about starting a family of her own, but it wasn't something she had wanted to rush into. She enjoyed her work and the sense of sharing it gave her with Brendan. Now, the decision felt very right to her. She was twenty-six years old and ready to be a mother.

When the clinic was over, she couldn't resist dropping by Tom's office to tell him her plans for the future. He could stop teasing her from now on, and start looking forward to being an uncle. She was grinning over the pleasure that would give him as she entered his secretary's office. Before she could inquire if Tom was free, Suzanne heard the raised voice of Leith Carew, its tone terse and angry.

"What's this about?" she asked the secretary.

A shrug and a helpless gesture pleaded ignorance.

Suzanne looked at the door into Tom's office. Every self-protective instinct urged her to leave right now, avoid any further involvement with Leith Carew. But anger meant he wasn't getting his own way, and he probably didn't realise that *his* way was not Tom's way, and never would be. If he was looking for trackers to continue the search for his niece . . .

Suzanne shuddered. Despite the police interpretation of the clothing found near the dingo's lair, she knew in her heart that if this was her family, she wouldn't give up, either, no matter what the odds against finding the child alive. She could well imagine the endless torture of wondering if enough had been done to find her. Not to have a decisive resolution would be very hard to live with.

Compassion fought with common sense and won. Or perhaps something else drew her to the door, something Suzanne did not want to recognise or acknowledge. She was aware of her pulse quickening as she turned the knob and pushed. Fear, she told herself, fear of how her life might be irrevocably linked to Leith Carew's.

As she stepped into the room Leith Carew's hand slammed down on Tom's desk. "What more do you want?" he thundered in frustration.

Tom's face wore the imperturbable look that was so deeply etched in his heritage, and Suzanne instantly knew that Leith Carew had inadvertently attacked values and beliefs that were sacred to her adopted brother, sacred to the ancient Pitjantjatjara tribe to which he belonged. Leith Carew could rage at him all day and Tom would maintain his ageless dignity, as little bothered by the other man's words as he would be by flies buzzing around his head.

He saw her in the doorway and rose from his chair to greet her. "Suzanne . . ."

Leith Carew spun around, the energy he was expending suddenly focussed on her, enveloping her with electric force. The initial incredulity on his face was swiftly replaced by a look of satisfaction as though her appearance in his life answered some question that had disturbed him.

I shouldn't have come in here. The thought flashed through Suzanne's mind. A ripple of panic coursed through her body as her gaze was caught and held by the man she didn't want to know. The feeling was stronger this time, the feeling that they had to mean something to each other. It must have to do with the child, Suzanne reasoned frantically. She couldn't let it be anything else.

She tore her gaze from his and quickly addressed her brother. "Tom, please do whatever is necessary to continue the search for the little girl."

He gave Leith Carew a look that clearly said the man had no understanding of what was involved.

"Do it your way," Suzanne urged. "Please, for me, for all of us. She's a lost child, Tom."

He knew what she meant. Each and every one of their brothers and sisters in the James family had been a lost child in one sense or another before being adopted. Tom was the only exception, and Suzanne was not sure the appeal would strike home.

No-one knew Tom's exact age. He had possibly been as young as nine or as old as twelve when he had been spotted alone in the desert by a scouting aeroplane for the Bureau of Mineral Resources. He had not been lost. He had been at home in territory that was familiar to him. But government welfare officers had subsequently found him and taken him to the Warburton Mission, believing it was for his own good.

There he had observed and despised how the ways of his people were corrupted by government hand-outs. When Suzanne's adopted parents offered him a home with them, Tom took the opportunity to get out of the mission, determined to learn the white man's ways, then use them for the benefit of his people.

He was doing a marvellous job of it, too, Suzanne thought proudly, but whether his commitment to his ancient culture would be swayed by the underlying ethos of the James family, a caring response to those in need, despite colour, race or creed, she truly did not know.

Leith Carew would never emit that kind of need to a fellow man. He was too arrogant, too inured in the power of his family's wealth. But Suzanne had not appealed to Tom for the sake of this man. It was for the child, the helpless, innocent child who was in the desert through no fault of her own.

Tom slowly nodded acceptance. "For you I will do it. What can be done will be done, Suzanne," he promised her.

She gave him a brilliant smile of relief, then without so much as glancing at Leith Carew, she stepped back and drew the door shut after her. She pushed her shaky legs into a brisk walk. The need to get away as fast as she could was not logical, if her only link with Leith Carew was to be the recovery of his niece, but Suzanne did not stop to analyse the feelings he stirred in her.

She heard footsteps running down the corridor behind her and didn't have to turn around to know who it was. Her heart pounded in panicky agitation. She hurried through the exit doors, fiercely willing Leith Carew to have second thoughts and go back to Tom. She had done all she could for him.

She was halfway to where her car was parked when he called to her. "Mrs. Forbes, please... would you wait a minute for me?"

It would be sixty seconds too long, Suzanne advised herself, yet her feet slowed as uncertainty clouded her mind. She did not want Leith Carew pursuing her to the medical centre. Better to deal with him here and now. Get it over with.

She stopped.

He caught up with her.

"I wish to ask you...thank you for what you just did."

Suzanne steeled herself to meet his eyes and challenge any claim he might make on her. "Mr. Carew. I didn't do it for you. It was for the child. I would have done it for anyone in such circumstances as these."

"Why did you come? How did you know? Rarely am I surprised, but when you came through that door, you just seemed to appear out of nowhere like an angel sent to ease despair."

"I'm not an angel, Mr. Carew, and I want to go now."

"You can't!" His green eyes warred with the guarded reserve in hers. "There's something special happening between us. I sense it. I know it."

"No. There's nothing. Nothing at all," Suzanne denied with vehemence, inadvertently revealing the inner turmoil he stirred.

"I've never been so drawn to any woman in my life before."

She flushed, guiltily aware of the attraction he exerted over her. "You mustn't say things like that. It's wrong."

She started to turn away. He grasped her arm to halt her. His fingers seemed to burn into her skin, making the heat of the day negligible in comparison.

"Do you love your husband?"

The question hurt. It jabbed totally unacceptable doubts into her mind. It squeezed her heart. She wasn't sure she knew what love was anymore. Only that being with Brendan had never been like being with Leith Carew. This was so physical, so immediate, so terribly strong. Not a quiet growing together with many mutual satisfactions giving a sweet and satisfying depth to their feelings for each other.

She felt a dreadful sense of betrayal in even hesitating over her reply. Her eyes flashed wild defiance at Leith Carew. "What I share with my husband is..."

"Come with me. Be with me. Let what's happening to us unfold in its own natural course."

The urgent passion in his voice threw Suzanne into more emotional upheaval. "Have you no sense of morality?" she flung at him accusingly. "Of knowing right from wrong?"

"Nothing like this has ever happened to me before. To let it go without exploring it..." He shook his head, unable to express the compulsion burning through him. His eyes seared hers with blazing determination. "I won't turn my back on it."

"Then I will," she bit out with equal determination. "Let me go, Mr. Carew. I will not be party to anything that hurts my husband."

She tried to pull her arm out of his grasp. His hold on her tightened. "You can't love him. I don't believe it. We were meant for each other."

"You don't know anything about me!" Suzanne cried, desperate to break free of this soul-tearing encounter.

"I know how I feel."

"And that's all you care about, isn't it?" she fired at him bitterly. "Never mind anyone else's feelings! Did you stop to wonder why Tom didn't respond to whatever you were offering him?"

He made a sharp dismissive gesture. Then as though struck by second thoughts, his eyes narrowed, and he asked, "Why did he respond to you as he did?"

She lifted her head proudly. "Because I'm his sister. And we share an understanding that you don't have, Mr. Carew."

"His sister?" Shock and puzzlement chased across his face.

"You see? You know nothing about me. Or Tom. Where we come from or who we are."

"I know you can't be any blood relation to him. Tom James is of the Pitjantjatjara tribe. I was told he lived in the Gibson Desert as a boy, and no-one knows it as well as he does."

"That's right! But you can't go over the heads of the aboriginal trackers who assisted the police. Tom wouldn't insult them by taking your offer. It's a matter of respect. And sharing. Your best course is to give a donation that will benefit the whole community, and let Tom organise the search with the others. There are rules and customs that you'll just have to be patient with if you want the best result. Listen to my brother and do as he says. And that advice is all I can give you, Mr. Carew."

"No. It doesn't end here," he insisted, shaking off the distraction she had hit him with.

"Yes, it does!"

"I won't let it."

"Brendan Forbes is the most decent man I've ever met. Last night I hope I conceived his child. Does that tell you how *I* feel, Mr. Carew?"

She saw the colour drain from his face. The intense conviction in his eyes glazed to a look of tortured uncertainty. The strength of his grasp on her arm slackened. She pulled free and propelled herself towards her car, her whole body churning against the threatened violation of the life she knew, the life she had made for herself, the life she shared with Brendan.

She reached the car.

"Suzanne...please..."

His voice tugged at her. She fought against it, clutching at the door handle, yanking it, uncaring that the hot metal scorched her fingers.

"I beg you to reconsider."

"No." The word was torn from her. "No!" she repeated vehemently as she opened the door and stepped around it, ready to get into the car. Then she looked at Leith Carew for the last time, firmly enunciating the only involvement she had with him. "I hope Tom can help you. I hope they can find the child."

Then she closed herself into her car and drove off.

It came as a shock when she found herself parking at the medical centre. She had no recollection of the trip across town. Not that it mattered now. She had arrived safely. And she had left Leith Carew behind.

Despite the oven-like heat of the car, Suzanne felt too drained to move. It was as though the encounter had sapped all her energy. She wished she could empty her mind of it. Wipe out the memory. Wipe out its impact on her.

She found herself wondering what might have been if she had met Leith Carew before she had met Brendan. A useless thought, with the unpleasant taint of disloyalty. She squashed it and pushed herself out of the car. A wave of dizziness caused her to sway. Her legs felt watery.

Get out of the sun, her mind dictated.

Get out of the heat.

Get on with your life.

CHAPTER THREE

AMY BERGEN WAS NOT FOUND.

Tom told Suzanne privately that the little girl had been taken from the scene of her parents' tragic deaths, but not by a dingo. He had tracked as far as two aboriginal camp sites. The search had been defeated by limestone outcrops that made it impossible to pick up any direction. Who had taken the child and where they were now, weeks after the last trace of them had been left behind, was impossible to tell.

No more could be done. Not even an army could find aboriginal nomads who didn't want to be found. The great outback held too many secret places for those who inhabited it.

A reward that ran into six figures was posted for any information that led to the recovery of the child.

Leith Carew left Alice Springs without making any attempt to see Suzanne again.

His departure lifted a weight off her mind.

EIGHTEEN MONTHS WENT BY, eighteen months that made devastating changes to Suzanne's life.

The joy of becoming pregnant was shattered by a miscarriage at three months. Suzanne became obsessed with conceiving again. Somehow having a baby was all important. She did not allow herself to dwell on why. Subconsciously she knew it was connected to putting the insidious memory of Leith Carew behind her and making an absolute affirmation of her commitment to Brendan.

She became more and more desperate and uptight about it as month followed month and it did not happen. Brendan persuaded her that she needed to relax and forget about getting pregnant for a while. He decided to take her on a second honeymoon.

They flew to Sydney for a quick visit to relatives and a shopping spree. The plan was to fly on to Brisbane, then over to one of the Whitsunday Islands near the Great Barrier Reef. They didn't make it past Brisbane.

Brendan became so ill on the flight that an ambulance was called to the airport to take him to the hospital. Suzanne could not believe it when the doctors told her he was a victim of a current variation of legionnaire's disease. That was something that happened to other people. She and Brendan didn't even live in Sydney. It had only been a brief visit.

Throughout her desperate worry over Brendan she was pestered by questions from health authorities who worked around the clock to pinpoint the source of the deadly bacteria. What shopping centres had they gone to? Had they stayed at a hotel? The bacteria was generally found in air-conditioning ducts or warm-water plumbing systems.

Suzanne answered automatically, questioning why she hadn't caught the disease as well. No-one could explain. The incident of the disease, compared to the number of people exposed to it, was minuscule.

The doctors couldn't make Brendan better. All they could do was treat the dreadful symptoms and ease the pain.

He died four days later.

Suzanne had stayed with him every hour she could, day and night, sitting by his bed, holding his hand, willing him to be one of the survivors.

It was her big American brother, Zachary Lee, who came to take her away. She couldn't accept that Brendan was dead.

"He's gone, Suzanne," Zachary Lee told her, wrapping her in his gentle bear hug, enclosing her in the warm security of the caring he had always shown her. "There's no more you can do."

Somehow his soft words crumpled the hard shell of disbelief she had clung to in the shock of her bereavement. Nothing seemed real anymore. Only the firm solidity of her big brother gave substance to the truth she had to face.

It was Zachary Lee who had found her all those years ago amongst the bewildering crowd at the Calgary Stampede, alone and frightened and crying her eyes out because she couldn't find her father. She clung to him now as she had clung to him then, a steady rock, emanating a comforting security that was totally dependable.

"I didn't love him enough, Zachary Lee," she sobbed in despair.

"Yes, you did," he assured her.

"No. You don't understand. I wanted a baby. We wouldn't have made this trip if . . ."

"Don't, Suzanne. You have nothing to blame yourself for. What happened was beyond your control. Anyone's control. Don't torment yourself with what might have been."

Zachary Lee talked to her for a long time. But it didn't help. It was one of those situations where no-one could possibly have foreseen the consequences, but in her heart of hearts, Suzanne had little doubt that if she'd never met Leith Carew, Brendan would not be dead.

The James family gathered to give their support to Suzanne, both at Brendan's funeral and in the weeks and months that followed.

Nothing helped.

Her sister Rebel and Rebel's husband, Lord Davenport, flew all the way from England to give her what consolation they could. Thirteen brothers and sisters of many different nationalities and backgrounds formed a cocoon of love and strength around Suzanne. The two people who had adopted them and welded them into a unique family remained close by, to be called on at any time.

There was a cold lonely place inside Suzanne that none of their warm caring could touch. She was grateful to them for being there for her, as she knew they always would be in times of need, but it did not make up for what she had lost.

The memory she held of Leith Carew became meaningless. Why did it take a disaster to reveal how much she cared for the man she had married? Brendan had been solid reality, Leith Carew a mere fantasy of what might have been in another time and place.

Her sister Tiffany and Tiffany's husband, Joel, invited her to stay with them in their beautiful home on Leisure Island. "You need someone to look after you for a while," Tiffany pressed, believing that her bright, optimistic nature could draw her sister out of her mental and emotional retreat from life.

Suzanne didn't want to, but somehow it seemed mean to refuse when they were being so kind. Zachary Lee also urged her to accept. The island was close to Surfers Paradise, not far from Brisbane, where he lived.

Tom promised to look after her home in Alice Springs. Suzanne was not to worry about anything. The family would take care of whatever needed to be taken care of.

She numbly agreed to the arrangements made for her. She was vaguely aware of days passing, weeks passing. Tiffany organised activities. Suzanne went along with them. But they were meaningless. The only persistent thought in her mind was the wish that she could go back and relive the past, particularly the last year, giving Brendan all the love she should have given him instead of being preoccupied with needs of her own.

She was plagued with guilt over the way she had let Leith Carew seed the compulsion to start a family. Even though nothing of substance had happened between them, meeting him had affected her. It didn't matter how many times she told herself that she had wanted a family anyway, she knew that if he had never walked into her life, it would not have become a matter of such urgency to her.

It was Tom who eventually rescued her from her morose apathy. He arrived at Tiffany's home one day and asked Suzanne to accompany him on a journey.

"Where?" she asked without any interest.

"To my homeland. It will heal you, Suzanne."

Despite her disinclination to make any concerted effort to do anything, Suzanne could not offend Tom by refusing his offer. She knew what a privilege it was to be invited to share a heritage that was unique to the people of his ancient tribe.

They flew to Alice Springs and Tom took her on a journey that was like no other she had ever experienced. It stirred her to taking an interest in learning to see through Tom's eyes, and she gradually perceived that what was uninhabitable desert to most people was a place that lived and breathed to a different set of rules.

They were sitting in companionable silence around their camp fire one night when Tom's head suddenly lifted, turned in quest of something Suzanne neither heard nor saw. Tom was unique. He could sense things that no other person, black or white, could feel, as though he was attuned to the vibrations and pulses of the universe.

She waited, aware of the listening stillness of his body, sitting absolutely still herself so as not to disturb his concentration.

The distant howl of a dingo carried faintly on the crisp night air. It did not strike any fear in her. Their camp fire kept the creatures of the wilderness at bay.

"Something's wrong," Tom murmured.

"What is it?"

"You don't feel it?"

"No."

But she knew he did. Tom's deep affinity with this vast outback land was in everything he said and did. Even the way he walked over it had a sensitivity that no white person could ever appreciate. He came from a race that for over forty thousand years had taken this country into their minds and hearts, sharing a unity with it that no newcomer could comprehend. At least, that was how Tom explained it. The primitive tradition of the Dreamtime was very real to him.

He rose to his feet in a fluid unfolding that had all the instinctive grace of a wild animal sensing danger. "Wait here. Keep the camp fire burning."

"Where are you going?"

"I don't know where."

"Why do you have to go?"

"A life has passed. Another life calls. It calls to me."

She didn't question any further, sensing his urgency to follow the call that only he heard. "Take care," she said, nodding her understanding.

A smile of assurance flashed from his dark face. She smiled her trust in him.

He swiftly became a shadow of the night, needing nothing but the moon and the stars and his own instincts to guide him wherever he had to go.

Suzanne slowly turned her gaze to the fire and released a long, pent-up sigh. Tom's softly spoken words lingered in her mind. *A life has passed. Another life calls.* They seemed to reflect her own situation.

Was there any meaning to life, she wondered?

Out here there was a timelessness that seeped into the soul. At night she could look at the brilliance of the stars and feel as though she was at the dawn of creation. By day, the sheer immensity of the landscape stamped a forever feeling in her mind, turning humanity into a mere speck of passing dust.

Yet even in this seemingly desolate world there was life, continually surprising her with its many fantastic forms. Without Tom to show her, she wouldn't have noticed much of it. He unfolded the secrets of the desert, sharing his intimacy with all there was around them.

Suzanne felt intensely privileged to be with him, aware that it was only because she was his sister that he was teaching her a new appreciation of the cycle of life and death, and that at the very heart of nature there was a necessary passing from one to the other. To Tom, it was only a shift in form.

The night air was chilly. From time to time Suzanne fed the fire as Tom had instructed. She stayed awake as long as she could, but when she found herself dozing off, she climbed into her sleeping bag and settled herself for the night. She had no way of knowing how long Tom would be. He might not be back until morning and he would not expect her to wait up for him.

He was not back when she woke soon after dawn. All day went by with no sign of him. She knew it would be madness to go looking for him but she couldn't help worrying. What was keeping him away for so long? She built a fire as the sun set, aware that he would expect it of her and would perhaps be looking for it after nightfall.

Suzanne knew she was in no personal danger. Their camp was by a permanent waterhole and she had plenty of food supplies. Tom, however, had taken nothing with him. She assured herself he knew how to survive in the desert and there was no need for her to worry. Tom would find his way back to her.

She ate a solitary meal, hoping that something else hadn't gone wrong, that there would be no other disastrous turn of fate to blight her life.

She woke frequently throughout the night, her sleep disturbed by the need to keep feeding the fire. During the long hours of the early morning, she kept a vigil, growing more and more afraid that her brother was lost to her.

Something was happening. Something of importance. Otherwise Tom would not have left her like this. Whatever it was, she felt the weight of another turning point in her life.

Another long day passed. Suzanne was now so worried that she seriously considered calling in help. Tom could probably look after himself better than any other man alive in this environment, but if he'd injured himself... It didn't bear thinking about. She busied herself with gathering more wood for tonight's fire. She was watching the sunset when she saw the movement far off.

Her heart took wing at the wonderful sight of a dark figure loping past clumps of spinifex, heading towards her. Suzanne began to run, unable to wait, compelled to assure herself that it truly was Tom and he had returned to her. As the distance between them diminished, she saw that he carried a bundle. His arms were cradling it against his chest.

"Are you hurt, Tom?" she shouted.

"Of course not," came the reassuring reply, a touch of scorn in his voice at the affront to his pride and dignity.

"What's kept you so long?"

"It was far away."

"I was so worried."

"I had to carry the child."

Suzanne rushed to meet him, to relieve him of the burden he had borne for the sake of the life that had called to him. The child was wrapped in a blanket. A little girl. Barely skin and bone. Asleep or unconscious.

"She's breathing," Suzanne said in relief.

"Yes. Given time and care, she will be all right."

"Who is she?"

"I don't know. She was alone with a woman of my tribe. An old woman whose life had passed. That was what I felt. Why I had to go."

How Tom could feel such things was beyond Suzanne's knowledge, but she had seen it happen before and she accepted it as normal. At least for Tom.

"The child is so fair. She can't be of your tribe. Nor of your race."

"That's true. But she needs food. We should give her something to eat."

They turned and walked to the camp site together. "It was good that you found her, Tom. If the old woman was alone..."

"Yes. The child would have died," he said with the emotionless resignation with which he viewed death. Suzanne was suddenly struck by a possibility that squeezed her heart. "Tom, we're over five hundred kilometres from the Gunbarrel Highway."

"That also is true."

He tipped some water into a mug and brought it to where Suzanne stood stock-still, holding the child with mounting emotion. It had been eighteen months ago. So far away. It couldn't be...

"Who is she, Tom?"

"I've had a long time to think about it. I knew the old woman, Suzanne. From when I was a boy. She was childless and always walked alone. Perhaps, to her in her old age, she believed the child was a gift."

He gently stroked the little girl's cheek. Her lashes slowly fluttered open. She had green eyes. Tom put the mug to her lips and let her drink sparingly. Although she obviously wanted more.

"But I think this is the child you asked me to find, Suzanne," he said quietly. "The one that was lost."

"Amy," she whispered. "Amy Bergen."

And the child looked at her with Leith Carew's eyes, as though the name struck some distant chord of memory.

The realisation came to Suzanne that her life was once more linked to the man who had refused to say goodbye to her. The man who had said there would be another time and place for them. She wondered if Leith Carew still thought about that. Whether he did or not, it was now inevitable that their paths would cross again.

CHAPTER FOUR

WITHIN HOURS of being notified that his niece may have been found, Leith Carew flew from Adelaide to Alice Springs to make an official identification.

There was little doubt in anyone's mind as to the outcome. None in Suzanne's. The photographs in the police file had been conclusive. The features of the child were the same as those of the two-year-old Amy Bergen, who had been lost eighteen months ago. Apart from which, she responded to the name, although her language was a garbled mixture of aboriginal words and pidgin English.

Suzanne heard the commotion outside her home when Leith Carew arrived, accompanied by the chief of police and other various authorities. Representatives of the media had been camped in the street ever since the news had broken. It was a big story and they intended to make the most of it, but the clamour of their demanding voices frightened the little girl, and she was Suzanne's first consideration.

Four days of travelling with Tom and Suzanne was too little preparation for the adjustment from a primitive life in the desert to the bewildering strangeness of civilization. The child was stronger now from their careful nurturing, but Suzanne was concerned about the mental and emotional upheaval that this experience might have caused.

She had clung to Suzanne like a limpet from the moment they had hit Alice Springs. Prying her loose for a medical check had been traumatic enough. Handing her over to an uncle she almost certainly didn't remember would undoubtedly be even more traumatic for her.

Suzanne tried to stay relaxed as Tom admitted the official visitors to her home, but she felt every nerve in her body tighten when Leith Carew stepped into the living room. He seemed to fill it with his strong presence, and Suzanne could not deny the tug of attraction she felt, despite all that had happened since they last met.

There was an immediate vibrancy in the air between them, an awareness that pulsed with memories and the possibilities of what might have been. Suzanne felt her skin tingle. Whether it was excitement or a sense of premonition, she didn't know. In her mind and heart was a recognition that this man was important in her life.

His green eyes held a look of reserve. He stood very erect, shoulders squared, body rigid, his face wiped of all expression. "Mrs. Forbes," he acknowledged her in the most minimal manner of greeting.

"Mr. Carew," she returned stiffly, her manner affected by the memory of how fiercely she had spurned any further connection with him, the cutting words of condemnation she had used, her violent dismissal of his feelings. And her own.

"It's kind of you to receive us here." It was a polite recitation, nothing more.

He challenged the interest in her eyes with a relentless impassivity, as though needing to prove to her and himself that she had no power to affect him any more. He was comprehensively armoured against any form of rejection from her today, Suzanne thought, telling herself it was only to be expected.

"We didn't want the child disturbed any more than she has to be," she offered softly, hoping to put him more at ease.

It was a vain hope. "So it was explained to me," he said, and in a pointed and deliberate dismissal of her, he dropped his gaze to the child cradled against her shoulder.

She, of course, was the prime focus of his interest, yet his attention seemed more directed at the way Suzanne had the child clasped in her arms. Suzanne had the distinct impression he would have preferred anyone other than herself to be involved in this situation.

A woman stepped up beside him, a tall, blond, beautiful woman who slid her arm possessively around his. It was not his sister. His only sister was dead. The woman was far too young to be his step-mother. The way she looked at Leith Carew evoked a weird little lurch in Suzanne's heart.

He glanced at the woman then returned a hard, glittering gaze to Suzanne. "This is my fiancée, Danica Fairlie," he announced. "Danica, this is Mrs. Forbes."

"How do you do?" the blonde said with polite formality.

Suzanne stared at her, stricken into silence by a sick feeling of hollowness. Fortunately her lapse in manners was covered by the chief of police, who broke into a speech about procedure, giving her time to pull herself together.

It was madness for her to feel so let down, so screwed up inside. Was this how Leith Carew had felt when she had thrown her love for Brendan in his face?

Yet nothing had really happened between them. There was no reason in what he had felt back then, no reason in what she felt now. Whatever passion-ate desire Leith Carew had once felt for her was gone. Had to be gone. He was probably embar-rassed by the memory of it.

A lot could happen in eighteen months, she re-minded herself savagely. A child who was lost could be found. Births, deaths and marriages could take place.

Danica Fairlie was not his wife yet, some fierce little voice inside her argued, but her eyes told her that the beautiful blonde was custom-made for a man like Leith Carew. The plain truth was that the child was the only real link between them, a transitory link that would soon be severed.

Suzanne valiantly tried to cling to this reasoning, but when Leith Carew stepped towards her, she felt her pulse quicken, and there was no ignoring the fact that time had not diminished the power he had to affect her thoughts and feelings. Nevertheless in these circumstances she had no choice but to do her utmost to repress her reaction to him. Above all else she had to consider the child in her arms.

As her uncle approached, the child buried her face in the curve of Suzanne's neck and shoulder. Her thin little arms took on a stranglehold. Leith Carew did not try to shift her or turn her towards him. Suzanne had asked one of her friends to buy a few clothes for the little girl, and all Leith Carew did was to gently push the loose cotton dress from the child's right shoulder.

Her skin was darkly tanned from the life she'd led in the desert, but there was a small discolouration on the curve of her shoulder, a reddish mark, vaguely shaped like a key. Suzanne had not noticed it before, not even when she'd bathed the child. It did not stand out. Yet if one knew to look for it, as Leith Carew did, it was clearly discernible.

"Amy," he murmured, and for one long moment of intimate sharing, his eyes locked with Suzanne's, revealing the anguish of all the lost months of his niece's life. Then he tore his gaze from hers and turned to the chief of police. "It is Amy," he stated decisively.

"Oh, Leith!" His fiancée stepped up to touch his arm, her face alight with relief and pleasure that the long ordeal for him and his family had come to a happy end. "How wonderful!" she cried, her voice husky with emotion.

The show of obvious intimacy with him cramped Suzanne's stomach, but she somehow managed to keep an impassive face.

It seemed to take a conscious effort for Leith Carew to make his face relax into a semblance of a smile as he looked at his fiancée. The emotional strain of the last few hours must have been intense, Suzanne reasoned.

"Yes, it is. Wonderful!" he repeated, then turned his attention to the child, the desire to take her from Suzanne and enfold her in his arms implicit in his eyes. Very gently he slid his hands around her rib cage, laying claim to her.

Amy's reaction to his touch was instant and violently negative. Her body squirmed in rejection. Her legs wound around Suzanne with an animal-like instinct to cling fiercely to the only safe support she knew. Her head burrowed farther into Suzanne's neck, hiding under the dark wavy mass of Suzanne's hair.

Leith Carew snatched his hands away as Amy's movement pushed them into contact with Suzanne's breasts. "What's wrong?" he rasped, his eyes flaring some indefinable accusation at Suzanne before he swung them to the chief of police. "You said she was fine. That she only needed a program of good nutrition."

"She's frightened, Mr. Carew," Suzanne answered flatly. "This is all so strange for her. Strange people. Strange noises. It's not the environment she's used to. She needs time to become familiar with it."

"Time..." He bit out the word as though it was an instrument of torture, and there was a savage derision in the eyes he turned to Suzanne. He looked bitterly at her hand as it moved to soothe the child with loving caresses. "She accepts your touch."

"I've nursed her all the way back to here, Mr. Carew," Suzanne explained.

"She belongs with me," he said with what sounded like jealousy.

"Now she does. But it was only a few moments ago that you identified her," Suzanne reminded him.

"Then tell her it's all right to come to me. Tell her I'm her family."

"She won't understand that, Mr. Carew. I'm sorry, but you'll have to be patient if you don't want to frighten her any further. She needs to be gentled into acceptance, not abruptly taken.''

His eyes warred with hers for several seconds before the emotional conflict inside him subsided into resignation to her reasoning. Suzanne knew that his tension, and the tension his nearness evoked in her, was not helping the situation. Perhaps he realised it, too. He made another visible effort to relax.

''So how do you suggest this is best handled, Mrs. Forbes?''

It almost killed her to say it, knowing that it meant spending more time with him, but her sense of responsibility towards the little girl left no alternative. ''There are too many people in the room,'' she said flatly. ''If it was only you here, and we could sit down quietly and give Amy time to let curiosity get the better of fear, it would be a start in the right direction.''

''A start,'' he repeated grimly.

''It isn't easy for her, either,'' she told him bluntly.

He relieved his inner frustration with a long, heavy sigh, then turned to the chief of police. ''What is the official procedure now?''

''Well, I'll need you to come down to the station. There are forms to be filled out and signed.'' He nodded towards Tom. ''And the business of the reward to be settled.''

''Of course!'' Leith stepped over to Tom and shook his hand with great vigour. ''I'm very grateful to you. I'd given up hoping we'd ever see Amy again. How you found her..." He shook his head in bemused respect for Tom's abilities. "I'd like you to tell me about it."

"You have my sister to thank, Mr. Carew," Tom said, very much on his dignity.

Leith Carew shot a dark frown at Suzanne. "But I was told..."

"It was Tom who found her," she stated firmly. "I had no hand in it."

"But for you, I wouldn't have been there to find her, Suzanne," Tom argued stubbornly.

"I want no part of the reward, Tom," she said with rigid determination, not wanting to take anything that would remind her of Leith Carew. She appealed to Tom's ingrained belief in sharing. "Use it for the good of your people."

Her brother's answering smile accepted that principle and expressed his pleasure in her giving. The argument was dropped.

Leith Carew looked frustrated with their quick settlement of questions that were still unanswered for him. "Chief, I'd be obliged if we can all go down to the police station now and get done whatever needs doing as fast as possible," he said with determined purpose.

"As you wish, Mr. Carew," came the ready agreement.

"Then if it's all right with you, Mrs. Forbes, Danica and I will return for Amy."

Suzanne nodded her agreement. As much as she recoiled inwardly from this arrangement, she could see no other way of getting the result they all wanted, for Amy to go willingly to her uncle.

"We'll try not to inconvenience you any longer than is necessary," he said brusquely.

"I would happily look after any child who needed care, Mr. Carew," Suzanne replied with a flash of pride. "It's no inconvenience to me."

Colour slashed across his cheekbones. "I didn't mean to offend, Mrs. Forbes, or slight your kindness and goodness of heart in any way. I deeply appreciate all you've done for my niece, but I realise that caring for her must have taken your time and attention away from your own child."

It was like a barb of pain slicing through her whole nervous system. Suzanne had no idea what showed on her face, but Tom moved like lightning to stand at her side and curl a comforting and protective arm around her shoulders, ready to give any support she needed.

The truth was she had loved caring for Amy and was dreading the return of the lonely emptiness that the child had filled. Giving her up, as Suzanne knew she must, was heart-wrenching enough without being reminded that she had lost the child that would have been hers.

And Brendan's.

Tears pricked her eyes and she swiftly dropped her lashes to veil the sheen of moisture. Her

thwarted maternal instinct urged her hand up to
stroke Amy's hair. "I have no child, Mr. Carew,"
Suzanne forced herself to say. "There is no need to
be concerned about my time. However long it takes
for Amy to get accustomed to you, that's fine with
me."

The effort to speak calmly and rationally left
Suzanne trembling. Tom's arm tightened around
her. The silence that followed her short speech was
rife with tension. Somewhere in the back of her
mind was the knowledge that Leith Carew hated
being with her, hated having to come back and be
with her again. It was a hatred so deep and violent
that it affected his judgment of what was right for
Amy.

Suzanne could feel more tears welling up behind
her eyes. Why did he hate her so much if he loved
Danica Fairlie? It wasn't right. Or what she was
feeling was wrong. She couldn't bring herself to
look at him. Couldn't look at anyone. She was
hurting too much.

It was Danica Fairlie who broke the tense im-
passe. "Thank you, Mrs. Forbes," she said quietly. "We're very grateful for your understanding
of what Amy is feeling. Perhaps if we buy some
toys, Leith. A doll..."

"Yes. I'm sorry. I..." His voice was strained,
jerky.

"It's difficult for you, I know," his fiancée said
with tactful sympathy. "I'm sure Mrs. Forbes will

do her best to prepare Amy for our return. Let's go to the police station now, Leith."

He cleared his throat. "Mr. James, if you wish to stay with your sister..."

"Yes," Tom cut in firmly.

"You'll be here when we return later?"

"You can count on it, Mr. Carew," Tom said with a vehemence of feeling that was uncharacteristic of him. "Miss Fairlie is right. It is best that you all go now. Please."

The chief of police immediately took on the role of usher and he had everyone out of Suzanne's home with admirable briskness.

Tom steered Suzanne to one of the sofas and sat her down. With the sensitivity that was uniquely his, he let her weep out the grief for all she had lost, aware that no word or touch could soothe the deeply personal hurt. He distracted Amy by softly talking to her in the language she understood and gradually coaxed her into releasing Suzanne and going to him.

Suzanne slowly recovered her composure and gave him a wobbly smile. "I'll be fine now. Thanks, Tom."

His dark liquid eyes burrowed straight through her brave facade. "It is very clear to me, Suzanne. Leith Carew is the cause."

She shook her head, shying away from the truth Tom saw. "Everything just got to me all in a rush. If Brendan and I had had the child we wanted..."

"Suzanne, there was bad feeling in this room. It was very strong. It made me remember that day in my office."

"What day?" she asked with false brightness.

"The day he was there. When you asked me to find the lost child," Tom replied patiently.

"You know why I asked," she defended.

He shook his head. "There was more. It flowed between you and him. A bright light with dark shadows. I did not know what it meant, but I saw it again today. And felt the pain."

There was no evading the knowledge in Tom's eyes. How he knew or saw or felt these things Suzanne couldn't even begin to guess. "I didn't do anything wrong, Tom," she pleaded.

"I know. It is not in your heart to do wrong. But he dimmed the shining in you, Suzanne. I do not want him to draw you into his darkness again. It is best that we work with Amy now. Have her ready and willing to go with him. Then it may change."

"May?" She gave a rueful little laugh. "You can't give me a guarantee, Tom?"

He frowned. "It cannot ever be told when something is over. There is always a flow that continues."

She remembered Leith Carew's passionate claim after they had left Tom's office.

We were meant for each other.

Perhaps in another life, Suzanne thought miserably. In this one she had married Brendan. And

Leith Carew was going to marry Danica Fairlie. Once Amy went with them, that would be the end of what might have been.

At least with a definite cutting-off point, she might be able to get on with living purposefully again, go back to nursing and help children like Amy come to grips with their lives. She heaved a deep sigh, then leaned over and stroked the little girl's hair.

"We'll soon be saying goodbye," she murmured. "Then it will be finished."

"No."

Suzanne looked at her brother in puzzlement. "You said . . ."

He had the faraway look in his eyes that was totally impenetrable. "It is not finished. There is more," he said with implacable finality.

CHAPTER FIVE

SUZANNE HAD HERSELF well in hand when Leith Carew and his fiancée returned for Amy. What Tom meant by "more" was apparently as indistinct to him as it was to her, but Suzanne privately assumed it centred on this meeting. She hoped to make it as short as possible.

Leith Carew undoubtedly had the same idea. The hour he had spent on official business had given him time to take stock of the situation. From the moment he entered Suzanne's living room, he emitted a quietly mannered charm that was custom-designed to allay any fears Amy might have of him.

He sat on the sofa with Suzanne, the child between them. Danica Fairlie declined the armchair Tom pulled up for her and knelt down on the carpet in front of Amy. She had spent the time shopping and she produced an assortment of soft toys in the hope of capturing the child's interest and acceptance.

Suzanne had to give Leith Carew's fiancée full marks for intelligence. She had chosen outback animals that were familiar to Amy, a camel, a kangaroo, an emu. The gifts coaxed the little girl's curicsity. The real pièce de resistance, however, was the doll.

It had long black wavy hair and blue eyes with thick black lashes. Amy touched it wonderingly, then looked up at Suzanne. *"Belonga youpella?"*

They were the first words she had spoken in her uncle's hearing. The shock of the cultural gap he had to bridge with his niece was swallowed into a frown as he realised the difficulties he faced with communication.

"She's asking if the doll belongs to me. Because of its colouring," Suzanne explained. "You'll soon pick up the sense of the words she uses." Then she smiled at the child. *"Belonga youpella, Amy."*

A smile of shy delight lit the little girl's face. It wiped away her uncle's frown. Suzanne saw his whole expression soften into one of yearning love as he reached over to touch his niece's hand. Amy did not pull away this time. She stared at his eyes, seeing that they were the same colour as hers, just as Suzanne had told her.

"It's Leith, Amy. Leith," he repeated, looking for some spark of recognition.

She shrank back against Suzanne, unsurc of what was expected of her. Danica Fairlie produced a musical box and handed it to Leith to play. The sound attracted the child into wanting to find its source. While Amy was still fascinated by it, Suzanne took the opportunity to remove herself from the scene.

"*Mepella makim tucker,* Amy," she said, using the child's words for getting food.

It brought a frightened look of uncertainty to her face, but as Suzanne left the sofa, Tom quickly took her place, reassuring Amy that she was not to be left with strangers.

It was a plan that Tom and Suzanne had agreed upon in the hope that Leith Carew could seize the advantage of her absence to form a bond with the child. They had done all they could to impress on Amy that she belonged to the man with the green eyes, but it was difficult to know if she understood the concept of family.

They had told her the story of her real parents but it clearly held no relevance to her. That life had been supplanted by her subsequent life. As far as Suzanne and Tom could tell, only her name remained from it.

The old woman of Tom's tribe who had saved and taken Amy as her own had apparently talked to the child in a natural way about her dying before the inevitable had occurred. There was no sense of grief over Gangan, as Amy named her. Whatever affinity she had shared with the old woman appeared to have been unshakably transferred to Suzanne. Which was unfortunate, but natural enough in the circumstances.

As Suzanne moved around her kitchen, preparing a tray of cold drinks and slicing up a banana cake, she kept telling herself there had to be a natural affinity to close blood relations, and given enough time with Leith Carew, Amy would surely feel drawn to him.

"Can I help?"

The offer startled Suzanne. She had not expected Danica Fairlie to follow her out to the kitchen. An uncharacteristic pang of envy stung Suzanne's heart as she looked at the woman whom Leith Carew had chosen as his future wife.

Her Nordic colouring was enhanced by perfect skin and fine classical features. Her fair hair was perfectly groomed in a soft silky flow to her shoulders. The slim, elegant tall figure was shown to advantage by obviously expensive coordinated clothes. She truly was beautiful, and polished class from head to toe. Suzanne had no doubt she belonged to the same social strata as the Carew family.

"I think it would be better if you stayed with your fiancé and his niece," Suzanne replied. Her mouth curved in an ironic smile. "That is the purpose of my being out here."

The other woman nodded, her light blue eyes glinting appreciatively. "I can't compete with you, Mrs. Forbes. It's up to Leith to get through to Amy."

Suzanne frowned. "Won't you be helping him take care of her?"

"Not directly. He'll be taking her straight to his family home in the Barossa Valley. I live in Adelaide. So does Leith, most of the time."

"I see," Suzanne muttered, not caring to hear any more about their relationship. She opened a tin of biscuits and piled some on a plate.

"What happened between you and Leith?"

The blunt question stunned Suzanne into stillness. Slowly and warily she lifted her gaze to the sharp questioning in Danica Fairlie's eyes. "What do you mean?"

"You're a very striking woman. He reacts to you."

Suzanne could hardly deny it, but she did not want to go into the reasons for Leith Carew's feelings about her. "I think you're confusing me with the situation, Miss Fairlie."

"No. It's you. He reacted to you in a way I've never seen Leith react to any other person."

"Perhaps he associates me with a very bad time for him," Suzanne answered quietly.

"So, you have met him before." Danica Fairlie's eyes glittered with satisfaction, as though she had triumphantly elicited confirmation of her suspicions.

It piqued Suzanne. She had some trouble keeping irritation out of her voice as she replied, "We met briefly on two occasions."

"And what were they?"

Suzanne bridled against what felt like a cross-examination. Danica Fairlie was a guest in her house, and in Suzanne's opinion, she was abusing the hospitality being extended to her. It invited a very cold reply.

"The first time was when my husband gave Mr. Carew the autopsy reports on his sister and her husband. The second was when he asked my brother to take up the search for Amy after the official one was abandoned."

"That's all?" She sounded incredulous.

"That's all, Miss Fairlie."

What had happened in the car park was an extension of the meeting in Tom's office, and certainly none of this woman's business. Nothing had come of it anyway.

Danica Fairlie held Suzanne's gaze, challenging the truth and substance of her reply. "He was a changed person when he came back from Alice Springs," she stated, still questioning.

It came as a small shock for Suzanne to realise that the relationship between this woman and Leith Carew was of such long standing. They had to have been close for well over eighteen months for Danica Fairlie to have noticed some difference in his manner or personality. But what difference? Had Leith Carew been as much affected by her as she had been by him?

There was, however, another explanation, and Suzanne gave it. "I don't know if you've experienced the death of people you love, Miss Fairlie. It's not something one gets over easily. And worse still, the loss of someone who's missing, not knowing if she's dead or alive. It does affect people. Very deeply."

Danica Fairlie looked discomfited. "I had the impression," she said slowly, "that something else happened. Something beyond the family tragedy. There's a difference between grief and bitterness."

"It's my experience that grief can take many forms."

"Have you had so much acquaintance with it?" came the sceptical question.

Suzanne's violet eyes darkened to purple in anger. "Yes," she snapped.

It brought a grimace. "From being adopted?"

"I'm one of fourteen children," Suzanne fired at her. "All of us were adopted. I've seen grief in all its manifestations."

Danica Fairlie waited for her to elaborate on that theme, but Suzanne did not care for any part of this conversation and she was certainly not going to do anything to prolong it. She shut the tin of biscuits and put it on the shelf. When she swung around, the other woman was still scrutinising her as though knowing she was missing something and intensely frustrated that she couldn't put her finger on it.

"Don't you think Mr. Carew would appreciate your support?" Suzanne said bluntly.

"He'll get it. A hundred percent."

"So why don't you go back to him?"

"Because we'll never meet again, Mrs. Forbes. I'll be with Leith the rest of my life. This was the only opportunity I'll ever have to find out what happened."

"You have no cause to be jealous."

"It makes it so much worse when people act honourably. I prefer honesty."

"I don't know how to convince you..."

"You already have. But Leith is mine, Mrs. Forbes. I happen to love him."

"If he loves you, Miss Fairlie, you have nothing to fear from anyone," Suzanne bit out, her eyes flaring a challenge straight at the blonde.

Her chin tilted. "He loves me."

"Fine! Then stop wasting your time on me."

That got rid of her, but Suzanne was left trembling from the disturbing and distasteful confrontation. It took her some time to feel steady enough to carry the tray into the living room. She didn't want to face either Danica Fairlie or Leith Carew again, but Amy would be looking for her return with the *tucker*. Her non-appearance might disturb the little girl. There was no escape from seeing this meeting through to its necessary end.

Amy was actually giggling at her uncle when Suzanne entered the living room. He was playfully teasing her with the soft toys. Danica Fairlie was gracefully disposed on the carpet beside him, one arm resting possessively on his thigh, her beautiful face lit with a winning smile at Amy.

It was a good sign that everything was working well. Suzanne knew she should feel pleased about it, but the lead weight that settled on her heart defied all common sense. She set the tray on the coffee table, helped everyone to whatever they wanted, then settled back in the armchair that Tom had pulled up for Danica Fairlie.

Despite the relaxed air she was trying her utmost to project, Suzanne knew that her presence was sparking tension that was counterproductive to what they all wanted. Tom was worried about her. She could see it in his eyes. Danica Fairlie was conscious of Leith Carew's reaction to her. Most of the tension was coming from him, forcing Suzanne into an awareness of his every movement although she steadfastly evaded looking directly at him.

Her eye was caught by the sparkling solitaire diamond ring on the third finger of Danica Fairlie's left hand. Did he really love her, Suzanne wondered? Deep-down love? Or was he settling for a compatible marriage, a partner in life who would fulfil social needs and perhaps a desire for a family? He was in his mid-thirties. Had he simply decided it was time to take a wife?

Danica Fairlie had certainly been waiting for it to happen for a long time if they had been close before Amy was lost. He couldn't feel terribly passionate about her, nothing like the passion he had expressed to Suzanne outside Tom's office.

She clamped down on the memory that speared through her mind. That was eighteen months ago, when his emotions had been stirred by other things. For all she knew, Danica Fairlie was already living with Leith Carew in Adelaide, and passion did drift into something more secure and comfortable after a while. It had with her and Brendan. But then she had never felt as deeply affected by Brendan's presence as she did by Leith Carew's.

She squirmed inwardly at the sense of disloyalty to her husband, but the truth was the truth, however unreasonable or illogical it was. She barely knew Leith Carew. She doubted they had anything in common in real terms. His life was totally different to the life she had led. Yet she still could not dismiss what there was between them. Whatever it was.

"Mrs. Forbes..."

Even his voice tugged at something in her soul, deep, resonant, compelling. She had to look at him.

"I want to thank you again for all you've done for Amy," he said, and there was no doubting the throb of sincerity in his words. "Your brother told me how he found her, and about your journey back to Alice Springs. Without your nursing skills, Amy might not have recovered so quickly."

Nursing skills! Nothing personal in that little speech. There was no warmth in his eyes, either, Suzanne noted. Not for her. A steadily controlled reserve was stamped all over his face. Whatever there was between them, Leith Carew wanted it behind him. Now and forever.

She gave him a stiff little smile. "It's always good to see a child getting better, Mr. Carew."

"My family is looking forward to welcoming Amy home. I called from the police station to tell them the good news. I can assure you she'll be given the best of care."

Suzanne nodded, wondering why he should think she might doubt it.

"I have a car waiting outside to take us to the airport," he continued levelly. "A company plane is standing by to fly us home. I don't think Amy will be overly disturbed if I take her with me now."

To demonstrate the acceptance he'd earned, he smiled at Amy and enfolded her small hand in his. The child did not resist. She certainly looked quite taken by her uncle. Suzanne's heart grew heavier with the knowledge that the moment of parting had come.

The green eyes flicked to her one last time. "If you and Mr. James would accompany us out to the car, making it a natural move towards leave-taking..."

"Of course," Suzanne agreed, rising from her chair with as much grace and dignity as she could muster.

Danica Fairlie sprang to her feet, eager to put Suzanne out of her life, as well. Tom urged Amy off the sofa and Leith Carew kept her hand firmly enfolded in his as he stood up. They moved to the front door with Amy enveloped in the group. There was no problem until they emerged from the house. Anything natural from that moment on was impossible. The media pounced.

A wild melee ensued, photographers jockeying for position to take their shots, interviewers shoving microphones as close as they could, yelling questions, police officers trying to clear a way to the waiting car. Leith Carew swung Amy up against his shoulder and barged forward, Danica Fairlie fast on his heels. There was no posing, no answering of questions, no goodbyes. Within seconds all three of them were in the back seat of the car, the door closed, and the driver firmly ignoring the howling mob as he put the car into motion, gradually picking up speed as motorcycle police cleared the way in front of him.

For a few fleeting moments, Suzanne saw Amy at the back window, a frantic, frightened look on her face. Then she was pulled down out of sight. No more looking back. She was being taken swiftly and surely into a future that Suzanne had no part of. But she would be loved and well taken care of by

her family, Suzanne assured herself, and that was
the most important thing.

The car turned a corner and disappeared.

And that, Suzanne told herself, was the last she
would ever see of Leith Carew.

CHAPTER SIX

SUZANNE DIDN'T SEE Leith Carew. She heard from him. The very next morning.

The steady drill of a telephone call bored through her heavy sleep. She had a sweet sense of relief when it stopped.

It started again, taunting her into becoming more and more conscious of it. She wanted to ignore it, tried to ignore it, resentful of anything that broke the oblivion she had been so desperate for after hours and hours of lonely restlessness.

The noise wouldn't go away. In the end, she flung out an arm, fumbled the receiver from the bedside table and dragged it across the pillow to her ear.

"What time is it?" she slurred grumpily.

"I'm sorry to be calling so early in the morning—"

Suzanne frowned. It sounded like Leith Carew's voice. Had to be a dream.

"—but the matter is extremely urgent," the voice continued.

"Who is this?" It couldn't be him. Her brain was playing tricks on her.

"Leith Carew."

Shock cleared her mind in double quick time. Her eyelids flew open, and she jerked up to a sitting position. "Who?" she demanded, to make absolutely sure.

"Leith Carew, Mrs. Forbes," he repeated firmly.

"What's happened? What's gone wrong?" she snapped. The worst fears rushed into her mind. She would be the last person on earth he would call on unless absolutely driven to it.

"I'm calling for Amy's sake. She seems to be completely traumatised. Nothing we've tried can draw her out of it."

"Have you called in professional help? There are people..."

"This is important to me. I won't have Amy meddled with. You're the only one she trusts."

Suzanne remembered the last frantic look she had seen on the little girl's face, and a wave of sympathy swamped her heart. "Do you want me to speak to her on the phone?"

A deep sigh. "I doubt that will help, Mrs. Forbes. Unless you can tell her you're coming, and then come."

"You want me to come?"

"I believe Amy needs you with her. She won't eat. Won't speak. Won't respond to anyone. It's as though she's retreated completely inside herself. The only thing that means anything to her is the doll. She keeps hanging onto that like grim death.

If you remember, she thought the doll belonged to you."

"I see," Suzanne said slowly, taking in the seriousness of the problem. "Have you tried talking to her in a—"

"For God's sake! We've got a communication problem! Nothing we say means a damned thing to her!"

Particularly not if Amy was paralysed with fear, Suzanne reasoned. Otherwise they might have managed. "So what are you asking of me, Mr. Carew?"

"I want to hire your services for as long as it takes to get Amy settled and happy here. I realise this will take you away from your normal job, but if a hefty donation to the Flying Doctor service or the medical centre will cover any inconvenience..." A pause for a sharp intake of breath and a long expulsion of it. "Whatever it takes to get you here for Amy, I'll give, Mrs. Forbes."

He hated having to ask. Suzanne could hear it in his voice. But Amy was his first consideration, as she should be hers. It was wrong to be thinking she couldn't bear to be in the same household as him with Danica Fairlie at his side.

"I assure you this is all open and aboveboard, Mrs. Forbes," he said tersely, revealing his awareness of memories that sat as uneasily on him as they did on her. "If you'll let me speak to your husband, I'll explain the situation to him."

The painful irony of that request drove so deeply that Suzanne was incapable of an immediate reply.

"Mrs. Forbes?"

"That won't be necessary," she said flatly. Leith Carew wanted her help with Amy, and Suzanne couldn't deny a lost child whatever support she needed, no matter what the cost to herself. To do that would be a negation of all her adopted family stood for, a betrayal of what she had been given when she was a lost child. "I'll come and do what I can. For Amy's sake."

"I don't wish to intrude," he said stiffly. "Your husband is welcome if you wish to bring him with you. All expenses paid."

She hesitated, wanting to tell him the truth of her situation, yet reluctant to evoke any thoughts and feelings that he so clearly wanted laid to rest. Better to let matters lie as they were, she decided.

"That's not possible." The only sensible course was to adopt a purely business-like manner to get through what had to be done. "I presume you'll arrange transport for me," she added crisply.

"And anything else that needs doing to get you here."

"I don't need anything from you except transport, Mr. Carew. I can be ready to leave in two hours' time."

There was a short silence, then softly, "I expected no less from you. I'll have a company plane waiting at the airport."

Suzanne heard the click at the other end of the line, and the burr of disconnection that told her she should get moving, yet she was slow to return the receiver to its cradle. Those soft words, *I expected no less from you,* had curled around her heart and squeezed it into stillness. They suggested a respect, an esteem that she had not known she had drawn from Leith Carew.

Why? Because of her caring for Amy's welfare? Or did it go deeper than that? Back to when she had rejected the temptation he had offered and stayed faithful to her husband. And to her marriage. She recalled his cynicism about the lasting power of love. Had she changed that?

Danica Fairlie claimed that something had made him different. On the other hand, she had defined it as a bitterness, which surely had nothing to do with respect or esteem. Suzanne shook her head and pushed herself out of bed. There was no point in thinking about Leith Carew in any personal sense. Still, it was nice of him to have said that. It showed that he held no hostility towards her over what had happened between them. Which was as it should be. She had not wronged him in any way.

She showered and dressed and packed enough clothes for a week's stay. Suzanne had no idea how long it would take to settle Amy into the Carew family home. She wasn't even sure that Leith Carew's solution of bringing her in was the right one.

It might draw Amy out of her trauma, but what of the long term?

Somehow she would have to discourage the child's dependency on her. Leith would certainly do his utmost to help her in that, Suzanne thought ironically. He couldn't want to have her stay any longer than necessary. And Danica Fairlie would undoubtedly be one hundred percent behind him. A week at most, Suzanne decided. Then, if other professional help was needed to ease the problem, the Carew family could well afford it.

She rang Tom to let him know what had happened and what she was doing. It surprised her when he showed more concern for her than he did for Amy.

"Are you sure you can cope with this, Suzanne?" he asked, his deep gentle voice softly probing her heart. He knew, as her whole family did, that she hadn't been coping with life at all since Brendan had died.

"I have to go, Tom. You know I have to," she replied with a vehemence she hoped would show she had regained a sense of purpose, an important sense of purpose.

"I remember how much you wanted a child of your own," Tom said quietly.

Tears pricked at her eyes. "I know she's not mine. It's only for a week, Tom. I'll come home then."

"Suzanne..." She could almost hear Tom feeling his way towards saying something more. She held her breath, keenly aware of the perceptions that were uniquely his. Whether it was his natural reticence, or acceptance of what he saw as the inevitable flow of life, he chose not to express whatever had made him pause. He simply said, "Call me if I can be of any help."

Perhaps this development with Amy was the *more* Tom had sensed yesterday, Suzanne thought, relieved over the lack of further argument about her course of action. "Thanks, Tom," she said warmly.

One hour later, Suzanne was in the Carew company plane and flying out of Alice Springs. She tried to keep her mind off the man who now belonged to Danica Fairlie. There was no point in worrying about Amy, either, until she came face to face with the situation and could see for herself what needed to be done.

She watched the seemingly endless red landscape stretching out far below her, thinking of the varied reasons that took people to faraway places, changing the courses of their lives forever.

Without the building of the overland telegraph line between Adelaide and Darwin, there would have been no town of Alice Springs. With three thousand kilometres of harsh and mostly waterless land to cross, the site was marked for a telegraph station simply because it had a permanent river spring. Because it could also boast of being surrounded by remarkable rocks, gorges, saltpans, deserts and the ancient red ranges of Central Australia, the town was now a tourist draw to the whole world, attracting thousands of people yearly to its unique wonderland.

Suzanne imagined the Carew family wished the area had never been opened to travellers, that Amy's parents had never gone on their outback adventure. Nevertheless, it was impossible to turn back the clock. And where she was heading now was no less unique in its historical development.

South Australia was the only state in the country that had never been a penal colony. Its first inhabitants had all been free settlers, and it was a well-known fact that the Barossa Valley had initially been populated by people from Prussia and Silesia who had fled religious persecution in Germany.

The valley had been named Barossa—*hillside of roses*—after a winegrowing district in Spain. With its Mediterranean-like climate and soil composition, it hadn't taken the settlers long to discover the valley's potential for growing vines.

It was now one of Australia's main wine-producing areas, and another tourist draw, but a vast and civilised contrast to the outback. Only an hour's drive from Adelaide, South Australia's capital, with so many long-established and wealthy wineries, it offered everything any sophisticated taste could want.

The classy image of Danica Fairlie infiltrated Suzanne's mind, bringing with it the uncharitable thought that Leith Carew's fiancée would undoubtedly appreciate all he had to offer her as a husband. Her innate sense of justice then forced Suzanne to acknowledge it probably made the two of them very compatible. She had no cause to judge their relationship on what little she knew of either of them.

Except the way Danica Fairlie had questioned her yesterday afternoon hadn't felt right. Why do that if everything in the garden was rosy? Maybe Danica wasn't as sure of her man as she claimed to be.

On the other hand, Suzanne had to admit that if she had witnessed such tension between Brendan and another woman, she would have been disturbed by it. But never in a million years would she have tackled the other woman. She would have put her questions to Brendan. So why hadn't Danica put her questions to Leith?

Everyone was different, Suzanne reminded herself, and had different ways of going about solving problems. It would be foolish to attach any significance to what had happened yesterday. Leith Carew had made his choice of a partner in life, and it ill behove her to be critical of that choice. It was none of her business, and she had to make sure it remained none of her business in the week ahead.

Apart from which, the tension between herself and Leith Carew would undoubtedly ease with daily

familiarity. It was the memory of their highly
charged encounter that was distorting what should
be a more natural response to each other as people. A few days in ordinary circumstances and the
past would be put in its proper perspective, a brief
aberration that could be sensibly dismissed. If for
no other reason but for Amy's sake, a friendly atmosphere had to be achieved and maintained.

Having lulled herself into a reasonable state of
mind in preparation for the situation she was flying into, Suzanne concentrated once more on
watching the spreading country below.

The barren inland was finally broken by the
Flinders Ranges, which gave way to the great pas-
toral properties. Thousands and thousands of the
best wool-producing sheep in the world dotted the
landscape. Then came the more populated areas
closer to the coast. The plane started a gradual de-
scent and, sooner than she expected, Suzanne was
looking at the "valley of the vines."

They landed at a private airstrip. The pilot es-
corted Suzanne from the plane, carrying her bag for
her. Leith Carew was waiting to pick her up. He
stood alone beside a four-wheel-drive vehicle. There
was no sign of Amy or anyone else.

Despite all her fair-minded reasoning, Suzanne
only had to see Leith Carew again and her heart and
mind were shaken by a force that had nothing to do
with reason. *Why does he do this to me?* she railed
in silent anguish. *Does he feel it too?*

She eyed him warily as he moved to meet her. Somehow he was more *male* than other men, his strong physique even more pronounced this morning in jeans and a short-sleeved cotton-knit sport shirt that gave clear definition to his impressively developed muscles. His hard, handsome face looked drawn and tired, evidence of a stressful and sleepless night. His dark blond hair was slightly ruffled as though he hadn't thought to comb it.

A heavy-lidded gaze skimmed her appearance, the loose overblouse and cotton slacks designed for comfort, negating rather than enhancing her femininity. His lips curled into a mocking little smile that quickly turned into a dismissive grimace. When his eyes finally met hers, it was with a look of weary resignation.

"I trust your flight was comfortable," he remarked with somewhat stiff politeness.

"Yes." Suzanne did her best to ignore the nervous fluttering of her heart and directed a smile at the pilot. "Thank you."

Leith Carew took her bag and gestured towards the waiting vehicle. Suzanne fell into step beside him.

"No improvement since you called?" she asked, anxious to get this meeting onto its proper footing.

"I told Amy you were coming. She didn't appear to understand," he replied flatly.

"I'm sorry," she sympathised.

"Not your fault." He sighed and offered her a ghost of a smile. "I appreciate your coming to our aid. We all do. Amy is very special to us."

"I understand," Suzanne returned softly. The only grandchild, the only living reminder of his dead sister, the only girl left in the family. Of course, Amy would be very special and important to them.

Their eyes locked for a moment in deep and silent empathy. Leith Carew wrenched his gaze away as though it hurt. Suzanne turned her eyes blindly ahead, shaken by the strong pulse of emotion that had throbbed between them. It was natural in the circumstances, she argued to herself, yet she knew in her heart it was more than that.

They reached the big Land Rover, and Leith opened the passenger door for her. He stowed her bag in the back seat as she climbed in and settled herself. "Not far to the house," he remarked as he closed the door on her.

The quicker they were amongst other people, the better, Suzannne thought. When Leith swung into the driver's seat and closed his door, her tense awareness of him multiplied a thousandfold. "Where's Miss Fairlie this morning?" she blurted out, inadvertently revealing what was uppermost in her mind.

"Danica had to go into Adelaide to settle some business," he stated curtly. "She'll be back this evening."

He switched on the engine. His fingers curled around the steering wheel and gripped hard. For several moments he let the engine idle, as though his mind was distracted from the obvious purpose of driving her to his family home. He turned a grimly set face to her.

"You have no cause to fear being alone with me, Suzanne." He looked her straight in the eye with steady determination. "I assure you there'll be no repetition of what I once wished for."

A painful flush flooded up her neck and scorched her cheeks. "I wasn't expecting... You've got Miss Fairlie," she jerked out in acute embarrassment.

His mouth twisted. "Yes. Danica and I have our future planned."

"You appear... well-matched."

"The perfect match," he agreed.

"I wish you every happiness together."

"Thank you." Then with no pause or hint to prepare her for what was coming, he added, "I take it that you still love your husband?"

Her chin tilted defensively at the derisive gleam in his green eyes. "I'll always love Brendan."

"I wasn't expecting anything else," he assured her, then looked away.

The Land Rover started forward with a jolt as he pressed his foot hard on the accelerator. For several minutes the highly cultivated land they were driving through was a meaningless blur to Suzanne. Why hadn't she told him Brendan was dead?

That she was a widow and no longer beholden to anyone? She should tell him now, get it out of the way. Or would he interpret that as an open declaration of interest in him?

He'd found his *perfect match* with Danica Fairlie, Suzanne savagely reminded herself.

Endless and orderly rows of vines slowly registered on her mind, huge well cared for buildings that undoubtedly had something to do with winemaking or storage, everything meticulously neat and ultra-civilised.

Suzanne felt a mess.

A total mess.

The reminder of her marriage to Brendan tapped a soul-heavy guilt that flooded over the turbulent feelings Leith Carew evoked in her. It was horribly wrong, this unlooked-for and unwanted link between her and a man who should have no part in her life. She had told Tom she could cope, and she must for Amy's sake, but it was going to be a long, hellish week in the Carew household.

Nothing could come of it, nothing except pain. This wild compelling attraction was some mad aberration. Yet the need was there to reach out and touch the man beside her in a way that he had never been touched before, by any other woman.

The temptation burned through her whole body. She looked at him. She met eyes that held the same unbridled need in them. She jerked her head away. "You should be watching the road," she said stiffly. "Having come all this way, I'd like to arrive safely."

He gave a harsh laugh. "Then you can make your contribution to it."

"How?" she asked.

"Don't ever, *ever,* look at me like that again," he said with bitter passion. "You made your choice. And I've made mine."

CHAPTER SEVEN

SUZANNE DIDN'T SEE another thing until the Land Rover came to a halt. The abrupt cessation of movement forced an awareness of where she was and what she was here for. She had a brief impression of manicured lawns and beautifully structured gardens surrounded by magnificent trees. Before she could take a look at the house, her door was opened and her view blocked by a man who stood ready to help her out.

"Mrs. Forbes, I'm Rolf Carew. Good of you to come."

He had to be Leith's father, Suzanne thought, automatically taking the hand he offered her as she stepped down from the high cabin. "Thank you. I'll do what I can to help, Mr. Carew."

He was of similar height but more heavily built than his son. His hair was white but he carried his age well, his strongly boned face still handsome although somewhat fleshy. There was a strained look in the green eyes that searched hers in hope of answers.

"Anything you want or think is appropriate, just ask, Mrs. Forbes. It's a miracle we've got Amy back. We didn't realise..." He shook his head, clearly distressed by the outcome of his granddaughter's return. "My wife is with her," he said gruffly. "It means so much to Madeleine."

"Amy comes before Madeleine, Dad."

Leith's curt words were punctuated by the slamming of the Land Rover's rear door. He joined them, carrying Suzanne's bag. The hard look he gave his father spoke of family tensions Suzanne knew nothing about.

"I wasn't suggesting otherwise, Leith," Rolf Carew retorted with a touch of anger.

"Weren't you?" It was a derisive challenge.

"I wanted Mrs. Forbes to understand..."

"She understands about Amy. That's all she has to understand. Mrs. Forbes is not here to deal with Madeleine's problems."

"You know damned well..."

"Yes, I know damned well," Leith cut in with a violence that made Suzanne flinch. "Nothing else matters but Madeleine's needs," he continued bitterly. "Do you think Ilana wasn't aware of that when she wrote her dying wish out there in the desert? You think she had any doubt as to where your priorities lay?"

"Madeleine loved Ilana. She loves Amy just as much," Rolf stated vehemently.

"So do I. For who she is. Not as a substitute," Leith retorted with such coldness it sent a shiver down Suzanne's spine.

"What the hell do you mean by that?" his father spluttered.

"I will not let you use Amy to compensate your wife for the daughter she lost when you married her. I'll be taking Amy away from here as soon I can. And we'll be staying away. As you did. From Ilana."

Rolf exploded. "If I've told you once, I've told you a thousand times! As far as I knew, you were both being well looked after by your grandmother. I didn't know Ilana was so ill. She was my daughter. I loved her."

"Not as much as you love Madeleine," Leith returned venomously. "You didn't care enough to keep in touch while you went on your wild-goose chases through the United States. And all of it for Madeleine's child. No thought for your own."

"The circumstances were different, for God's sake! Madeleine's daughter had been kidnapped!"

Suzanne's gasp of horror at such a dreadful crime went unnoticed by the two men who were bullishly intent on locking horns until one or the other of them was forced to back off.

"Taken, not kidnapped," Leith corrected his father with pointed scorn. "And I imagine her ex-husband considered he had a right to his daughter.

I've often wondered how much guilt you felt about that."

"Why should I feel guilt?" Rolf challenged.

"You were taking her away. Putting the entire Pacific Ocean between that man and his child. He undoubtedly felt justified in claiming his own while he still could."

"He had no right. Madeleine had custody."

"Most two-year-olds are given to their mothers in a divorce action. That doesn't mean their fathers don't love them. He obviously loved her more than you loved Ilana."

Rolf looked at his son with soul-sickened eyes. "You don't understand. You never have."

"There's no similarity whatsoever to the way Amy was lost," Leith bored in with relentless logic. "If Madeleine is intent on seeing some parallel to her case, that's your problem. Not mine. Not Mrs. Forbes's. And not Amy's. So work it out between yourselves."

He took Suzanne's arm and drew her with him up the front steps to the portico that framed the entrance to the house. Still stunned by the fierce argument between the two men, Suzanne noticed little about the house. Her mind soaked in the impression that it was massive, built of sandstone blocks and double-storeyed, with wide verandas protruding from each floor.

"There's no mercy in you, is there, Leith?" his father shot after him in bitter accusation.

Leith's hand tightened on Suzanne's arm as he looked back. His face might have been carved to personify ruthless judgment. "The last thing Ilana did was to appoint me guardian of her child if Amy survived. *Her* daughter will be *my* daughter."

"You think Danica will make a better mother than Madeleine?"

The taunt must have caught something raw inside Leith. He lashed back with biting contempt. "Amy will have a father who won't desert her for someone else. She will always be able to count on *me* being there for her. Just as Ilana did."

Rolf Carew made no reply to that. For several moments the two men glared at each other, the silence seething with deeply rooted conflict. It was Leith who turned away, resuming his purpose of escorting Suzanne to the child who would be his from now on.

Leith's bitterness could not be attributed entirely to herself, Suzanne realised in some relief. Danica Fairlie was wrong about that. If he'd come back from Alice Springs a different man, there was far more behind that change than a rejection by a woman. His grief over the death of his sister had obviously been exacerbated by long-held family resentments.

She remembered Tom's foreboding words when he spoke of his perception of Leith—*I do not want him to draw you into his darkness.*

The *darkness* had been in Leith Carew before she met him. Suzanne was certain of it now. Maybe if circumstances had been different and she had been free to reach out to him then ... But that time was past. Leith had made *his choice* emphatically clear in the car.

She had a sick, empty feeling of defeat as he ushered her into his family home. "Don't you think I might be more effective if I knew what I'm walking into?" she asked.

His tight, set face remained tight and set. His eyes flashed with savage determination. "I'll make sure you have a free hand with Amy. That's all that need concern you."

Which effectively closed the conversation and shut Suzanne out of his life.

They entered an enormous foyer and headed for a magnificent mahogany staircase. Suzanne idly noted the parquet flooring, Persian rugs, some marvellous pieces of antique furniture against the walls. Old wealth, she thought, and wondered if it had brought any happiness at all to this family.

Broken marriages were hardly a recipe for happiness where children were involved. So often their love and loyalty were divided by warring parents, their emotional security torn apart. Custody battles were all too common.

Suzanne wished she knew what had happened to Rolf Carew's first marriage, how long it had lasted and what it had been like. There was little doubt his second marriage had raised many problems, however much he loved his present wife. Leith had spoken of the effect on his sister, but what about the effect on him?

Not that it was any of her business, Suzanne reminded herself, and Leith was not about to welcome any questions about it. They walked up the wide staircase side by side without a companionable word. So much for achieving a friendly atmosphere, Suzanne thought with dull irony.

Leith's relationship with his stepmother was undoubtedly as strained as that with his father, and Rolf Carew's comment on Danica did not smack of wholehearted approval. On the other hand, perhaps Rolf Carew's emotional bias towards his wife made any woman come off worse by comparison.

Amy's future with this family was beginning to look less shiny by the moment. The little girl was clearly the focus of various conflicts and could have sensed the undercurrents of emotional turmoil swirling around her. Perhaps that had contributed to her withdrawal.

As they reached another foyer-like area at the top of the staircase, Suzanne touched Leith's arm to draw his attention. "Was there an argument over Amy yesterday? In front of her?"

"You think I would allow that?" he snapped.

Suzanne withdrew her touch as though she had been burned. "I'm sorry. It seemed possible."

He closed his eyes against the appeal in hers, gave vent to a heavy sigh to relieve his inner tension, then offered an apologetic grimace. "No. *I'm* sorry. Your question was pertinent."

His eyes held hers in bleak acknowledgment as he added, "Amy's condition has nothing to do with any of us. It was leaving you that started it. The farther away we went, the less she responded. By the time we arrived here she had closed herself off from us. I doubt that anything said or done in this house has had any meaning to her."

Suzanne knew it was none of her business, yet she could not refrain from asking, "If I can bring her out of it, what then?"

"She'll have everything I can give her. All my sister wished for her."

Suzanne stared at him, deeply touched by the feeling he had revealed in those soft words.

His mouth twisted. "Where the rights of children are concerned, I have a very rigid belief that no harm be done to them. You have no cause for worry, Mrs. Forbes. I will look after Amy as though I was her father, and she my child."

"I wasn't doubting it," Suzanne assured him quietly.

"Thank you. Then perhaps we can move on." He led her down a wide hallway. "This is the children's wing. Amy's room has been kept precisely the way it was in hope of her return. It may jog some sense of recognition eventually."

"How long will she be here?"

"Until Danica and I are married."

"And when will that be?" The question slipped out before Suzanne could bite it back.

It earned a hard look. "It can't be too soon as far as I'm concerned."

"You haven't set a date?" Madness to persist with such personal questions, yet some dogged need to know overrode common sense.

"That will now depend upon Amy's progress. Danica and I have already discussed bringing the date forward to accommodate Amy's welfare."

"She doesn't mind taking on your sister's child?"

There was a gleam of derision in his eyes. "Danica is not about to say no to what I want. That's one thing *I* can count on."

One hundred percent, Suzanne recalled in self-derision. The stage was set, the players in place. Decisively cast as an outsider by Leith Carew, she had only one purpose here, and it was about time she focussed her mind on it.

"Amy's room?" she asked as he paused in front of a door.

"Yes. I'll handle Madeleine. You concentrate on Amy."

She nodded and he opened the door.

It was a beautiful little girl's room, furnished in pink and white with touches of lemon, soft feminine frills on the window curtains and quilts on the twin beds. There were shelves of picture books and every soft toy a child could desire. Mobiles of brilliantly coloured birds and tropical fish hung from the ceiling to delight the eye. It should have been a magical place for Amy, but she was curled up in a tight ball on the far bed, her face to the wall.

Beside her sat a woman, gently stroking Amy's hair. So absorbed was she in watching for, perhaps willing a response from the child, she did not seem aware that anyone had entered the room. Her yearning tenderness struck an instant chord of empathy with Suzanne, whose own thwarted need for a child had been too fleetingly eased in nursing and caring for Amy.

It must be worse to have had a daughter and lost her, Suzanne thought. She did not know the rights and wrongs of Madeleine Carew's first marriage, and could make no judgment on what had happened, but she imagined it was just as bad to be left wondering about a daughter as it was to be left wondering about a mother.

At least Madeleine Carew had her twin sons to console her. And a husband so devoted to her that she came first in his life. She was not alone as Suzanne was alone, with Brendan gone and no child at all to love from their marriage.

"Madeleine, Mrs. Forbes is here," Leith stated quietly but firmly.

Her hand stopped moving. With obvious reluctance she lifted her gaze from the child and turned her head towards them. Whatever her age, she was a strikingly beautiful woman, her soft feminine features enhanced by flawless magnolia skin and framed by thick wavy black hair liberally streaked with white. Her huge dark eyes seemed unfocussed for several seconds, their lustre dulled by a deep abiding sorrow that Suzanne sensed so strongly her own heart twisted in sympathy.

"If you'll move aside," Leith pressed impatiently.

A bleak look of resignation swept over her face as she stood up and stepped away from the bed. She said no word to her stepson, but as Suzanne moved forward, Madeleine's attention switched to her, fully alert and sharply appraising.

"It was you who found her?" Her voice had an American accent that reminded Suzanne of Zachary Lee's. A Southern lilt.

"No. It was my brother, Tom," Suzanne replied briefly.

"I knew it couldn't happen twice. God couldn't be that cruel. If only..."

"Madeleine!" Leith bit out her name in steely reproof. Exasperation threaded his voice as he added, "Please leave us. If you want to be useful, arrange some morning tea for Mrs. Forbes."

"Yes. Yes, of course," she agreed dispiritedly, her gaze flickering away from Suzanne. She cast one last yearning look at Amy, then walked stiffly from the room.

Leith closed the door behind her and heaved a sigh of relief. He gestured towards the bed where Amy was curled up in a world of her own. "It's up to you," he said softly, and for once there was a look of intense vulnerability in his eyes, begging for a resolution that he felt only she could give.

Suzanne was aware of her heart beating faster as she knelt on the bed and reached for Amy. So much love and so much pain were locked around the small child she had to rescue from wherever she had taken herself. Did love and pain go hand in hand?

She shook her mind free of such dark thoughts, knowing she had to give Amy her full attention. With gentle care she lifted the tightly coiled child onto her lap and began to rock her, talking softly in the language she had learnt from Tom.

Amy had the doll clutched against her chest, the hold reinforced and protected by her tuck position, knees drawn and head bent. Suzanne made no attempt to ease the child out of her instinctive self-containment. For how long she kept on rocking and talking, she had no idea. It did not matter. Only the child mattered.

Slowly, ever so slowly, the bent head began to stir, to lift. Eyelashes fluttered uncertainly.

"It's Suzanne, Amy. Suzanne."

The warmly repeated assurance was the final persuasion to look, to see. Amy stared at the face hovering over hers and recognition sparked. Her knees jerked down. Her arms flew up. The doll rolled onto the bed as Amy scrambled to cling onto the real live person it had represented to her.

"It's all right, baby. I'm here. I'm here," Suzanne crooned lovingly, wrapping the child in a secure embrace as little hands burrowed under her hair and Amy's face pressed into her neck.

In sheer blissful relief that Amy had responded to her, Suzanne swept a trail of fervently felt kisses over the silky head. Only then did she remember the man who had been waiting and watching for the response she had drawn from his niece. She looked up, wanting to share the moment with him, but there was no relief or joy on Leith Carew's face.

Pain looked at her, pain so stark and acute it pierced her heart and drove words of comfort to her lips. "Give her time, Leith. That's all it needs."

"The healer of all wounds," he drawled derisively. His gaze dropped to the discarded doll. "Except it doesn't. And substitutes come a poor second."

Suzanne didn't know what to say. Was he referring to his stepmother or himself?

"But I'm being ungrateful," he muttered, then made a visible effort to recollect himself, offering her a wry smile. "Thank you for giving Amy your magic, Suzanne. I'll go tell Madeleine that we might have a hungry little girl for morning tea, as well."

Magic... The word revolved around Suzanne's mind as she stared at the door Leith Carew closed after him. It was the word he had used in asking about her marriage to Brendan on the day they had first met. She remembered replying that her marriage wasn't based on magic, but maybe he had equated that word with the warm feelings of love.

Had Leith never felt loved?

What had happened to his mother?

Madeleine had clearly not filled that role for him. As for his father, any love between them had been lessened or eroded by the priority given to his second wife.

But what of Danica Fairlie? Leith had said he could count on Danica doing whatever he wanted. Wasn't that an expression of love?

Suzanne brushed her cheek over Amy's hair, deeply troubled and confused by the way Leith Carew tugged on her soul. Just as the child in her arms did, but in a different way. Perhaps Amy would fill the dark void in Leith's life.

The void in her own suddenly loomed larger and larger. Suzanne shut her eyes tight and resolved not to think about it. Take one day at a time. Work with Amy. Then she would go back to Alice Springs, to other children. That was the sensible thing to do.

Yet Suzanne could find no conviction in her heart for it. Her life felt as though it was in transit, waiting for the right connection.

There is more, Tom had said, but where did *more* end?

CHAPTER EIGHT

FROM LEITH CAREW'S telephone call early this morning it had been a long, energy-sapping day for Suzanne. Danica Fairlie's arrival on the scene did nothing to brighten the end of it. Not that Danica wasn't gracious about Suzanne's presence. Her polite and pleasant manner gave no cause for criticism. Yet her sharp observation of any passage of conversation between Leith and Suzanne was a gnawing source of tension that made natural behaviour extremely difficult.

Suzanne would have done almost anything to evade the formal evening meal arranged to celebrate Amy's return to the family, but circumstances conspired to trap her into it.

Despite being given an earlier nursery tea, Amy was far too excited to settle down for the night. Suzanne's suggestion that she stay with the child and for a meal to be sent up to her was firmly vetoed. She deserved to relax after all she had done. The general consensus was to let Amy stay up and join in the family gathering.

Since Amy's acceptance and familiarisation with her new life had to be the first consideration, Suzanne could hardly protest the decision. Cold, hard common sense insisted that the sooner the little girl became adjusted to it, the sooner Suzanne could take her leave of the Carew family, satisfied that her job was done.

However, Suzanne had little doubt it was going to be a very hollow satisfaction, with no joy in it. There was certainly no joy for her in joining the Carew family for dinner, although in some other place, at some other time, and in other company, she would have been charmed by the elegant dining room and the hospitality extended to her.

Superbly prepared food was served on Royal Doulton china. The finest wines from the Carew cellars were poured into glasses of Baccarat crystal. The silverware shone so brightly it was reflected in the highly polished mahogany table. It was the ultimate in sophisticated living.

And Suzanne was left in no doubt Danica was accustomed to this lifestyle.

"You set such a beautiful table, Madeleine," she enthused. "Did I tell you my father is in Ireland at the moment? He's promised to buy me a complete set of Waterford crystal." She turned to Leith. "What pattern do you like best, darling?"

"You choose, Danica," he said. "I always admire your taste."

"Thank you, Leith."

She stroked his arm with her perfectly polished fingernails. Laying possessive claim to him, Suzanne thought, then forced herself to acknowledge it was a perfectly natural gesture of affection.

Danica and Leith *were* suited to each other. The perfect match, as Leith had claimed. But confirmation of that fact did nothing for Suzanne's appetite. Nevertheless, she set herself to doggedly eating the food placed in front of her, desperately wanting the meal to be over. She was an outsider here, and Danica made her feel more and more of an outsider in talking about things that only the family circle were acquainted with.

It was some relief that the atmosphere at the table was not as unpleasant as Suzanne had expected it to be, given the family tensions. Rolf Carew sat directly opposite Suzanne at the other end of the oval table. His pride and joy in his twin sons, Jeb and Stuart, were as obvious as his love for Madeleine. Whenever he looked to his right, where all three were seated along the table, his expression softened with pleasure.

To his left were Danica, Leith and Amy. Danica received faultless courtesy from him. He was on guard with Leith. Only his grandchild drew kindly attention from him on that side of the table, but even that was fairly restrained, caution keeping him from intruding on Leith's declared territory.

Jeb and Stuart were clearly Madeleine's sons, with their wavy black hair and dark shiny eyes, yet there was enough of their father in them to show a resemblance to their much older half-brother.

The easy rapport they shared with Leith surprised Suzanne, although, on second thoughts, she realised that Leith was not the kind of man to visit the sins of the parents upon the children. To the twins he was very much their big brother whom they admired and respected, and he treated them with friendly affection.

His manner to Madeleine was not without kindness, Suzanne had noted, although he firmly controlled whatever he saw as over-emotionalism towards Amy. With his father he kept an armed truce, but it was all too apparent that war between them would break out again if there was any incursion on the line Leith had drawn for the future of Ilana's child.

Leith's manner to Suzanne was the same as Rolf's to Danica, faultless courtesy. The moments of intimacy Suzanne had known with him this morning might never have been. He was clearly as intent as Danica on demonstrating that his *choice* was made. Yet Suzanne could not help tensing in some instinctive anticipation every time he glanced her way.

Eventually the main course was cleared away and cheese and fruit were placed on the table. Suzanne wondered if she could reasonably excuse herself and take Amy upstairs to bed. The little girl was at last showing signs of wilting in the highchair that had been set for her beside Suzanne.

"Hey, Amy! Watch this!" one of the twins commanded with an appealing grin.

He chose a strawberry from the silver platter of summer berries, tossed it up in the air, and his brother caught it in his mouth. Amy watched wide-eyed as the trick was repeated the other way around. Then both twins held their strawberries between their teeth as a finale to the double act.

"Boys! You are at the table," Madeleine chided, but there was a note of indulgence in her voice.

Jeb and Stuart were refreshingly normal teen-agers, exuberant and uninhibited in welcoming Amy back into the family. Since their arrival home from high school, they had helped immeasurably in drawing the little girl out of her shyness, and Suzanne was intensely grateful for their bright presence. It was a welcome distraction from the togetherness that Danica was continually pressing with Leith.

Both boys ignored their mother's reprimand, biting into the juicy fruit with exaggerated relish and rolling their eyes at Amy to show how good it tasted.

"Give her one, Mrs. Forbes," Jeb urged. "Bet she'll try it now."

The twins had set themselves to coaxing Amy into tasting what was strange food to her, and they had been engagingly successful at it.

Suzanne gave her a strawberry.

Amy nibbled at the fruit experimentally, then chewed it up with pleasure. The twins grinned at her and she grinned at them. They repeated their trick with raspberries and blueberries, making everyone smile at the novel way of persuading Amy to eat what they were eating.

Suzanne was conscious of Danica growing impatient with the boys' act. Leith was giving most of his attention to Amy, who sat between him and Suzanne. The little girl's dependence on Suzanne, always looking to her for reassurance and encouragement, was undoubtedly an irritant to Danica since it meant Leith's attention was drawn to Suzanne, as well.

None of Danica's attempts at currying favour with Amy had met with any marked success. Sensing the other woman's mounting frustration, Suzanne was not surprised by the broad hint that came her way.

"You must be tired, Mrs. Forbes," Danica remarked in a sympathetic tone, having noticed that Suzanne had not bothered partaking of the cheese or fruit.

Suzanne managed a smile at her. "Yes, I am," she acknowledged, knowing full well that Danica wanted to see the back of her so that she could have Leith to herself.

Since the opportunity had been handed to her, Suzanne pressed her own purpose, her gaze running around the table as she spoke. "Thank you for your generous hospitality. It was a lovely dinner, Mrs. Carew. But if you don't mind..."

"Coffee is about to be served," Rolf interrupted invitingly.

"No, thank you, Mr. Carew. I think it's time to settle Amy down for the night, and I'd like to retire myself. If you'll excuse us?"

As she rose from the table both Rolf and Leith started out of their chairs, as well. "Please don't get up," Suzanne put in hurriedly, anxious to evade another open clash between the two over Amy's welfare. "I think it will be easier if you simply say good-night to Amy here, without fuss."

No-one argued. It was well past Amy's normal bedtime. The two men sat down again in acquiescence to Suzanne's knowing what was the best course of action.

She picked Amy up and held her against her shoulder as good-nights were chorused around the table. It delighted everyone when Amy shyly repeated the word. Suzanne was about to carry her off when she remembered something else she wanted to do. She quickly addressed her host at the head of the table.

"Mr. Carew, I'd like to call my brother Tom and let him know about Amy. Is it all right for me to telephone Alice Springs?"

"Call anyone anywhere, my dear. After what you've done for Amy—" he gestured with open hands "—we are deeply in your debt."

"Your husband must be waiting on a call, as well," Danica put in sweetly. "It was very good of him to lend you to us when he must need you on his staff at your medical centre."

"I imagine Dr. Forbes is well acquainted with emergency flights," Leith said, lifting his glass of sauterne from the table and leaning back in his chair. He raised flat green eyes to Suzanne. "But do please pass on our gratitude to him, Mrs. Forbes."

However inappropriate the time was, Suzanne could no longer allow this misconception about her marital state to go on. She felt a flush of embarrassment sting her cheeks as she formed the necessary reply.

"I can't call my husband," she started, her voice husking over the welling lump of emotion in her throat.

"Oh? Is he off somewhere with the Flying Doctor service?" Danica inquired brightly.

Suzanne shifted her gaze to the woman who was so determinedly intent on shafting the point of her marriage into everyone's consciousness. Hadn't she already made enough points about her relationship with Leith tonight?

The glitter of satisfaction in Danica's sharp blue eyes stirred an anger in Suzanne that overrode her pain at having to speak of Brendan.

"No, Miss Fairlie," she said coldly. "My husband is dead."

The blunt declaration caused a shocked stillness around the table. Suzanne saw a number of expressions flit across Danica's face. Satisfaction was not one of them. Suzanne felt no satisfaction, either. Her anger died a quick death as the memory of Brendan's four days of dreadful suffering swept into her mind and cramped her heart.

The sound of shattering glass broke the frozen tableau.

"Leith! Look what you've done!" Danica gasped, half rising, dabbing at her dress with her serviette.

It was as though he didn't hear her. His face was a tight strained mask, his eyes ablaze with turbulent emotions focussed entirely on Suzanne as he rose to his feet. His chair scraped back, tipped, crashed onto the floor, scattering shards of crystal.

"Leith!" Danica screeched in protest. "Watch what you're doing!"

It fell on deaf ears. "I'm so sorry, Suzanne," Leith said in a tone of pained regret. "How did it happen? When?"

All the agony and desperation of those terrible hours beside Brendan's hospital bed came back to her. Tears swam into her eyes. "Twelve weeks ago. Twelve weeks and three days," she recalled brokenly.

He looked as agonised as she felt. "He was a good man. A caring man. One of the best."

"Yes. Yes he was," she whispered. Then, because it seemed terribly important to say it, she added, "I loved him."

"I know you did, Suzanne," Leith assured her softly. "He couldn't have had a finer wife."

Somehow this quiet accolade eased her inner anguish. Leith understood. It was right for her to have loved Brendan. There was no longer any sense of tension over what had happened between her and Leith in the past. She felt his approval of the stance she had made over her marriage. More than approval. There was caring in his eyes, a deep caring, reaching out to her and wanting her to accept it.

"I'm sorry, too."

Danica's brusque words sliced into the moment of acceptance.

She moved to stand beside Leith, her eyes flashing both fear and aggression as she curled her arm around his, ensuring they both recognised her position in his life. "If I'd known about your recent bereavement . . ." She gestured apologetically with her other hand. "Please forgive me, Mrs. Forbes."

Suzanne became aware of the rest of the Carew family watching, enthralled by the unexpected play of emotion between her and Leith. Danica's move heightened their interest even further. Eyes were working overtime, glances darting at the three of them. Amy stirred restively in her embrace, reminding Suzanne of her intention to put her to bed.

Feeling hopelessly self-conscious about having caused such a provocative scene, Suzanne quickly nodded acceptance of Danica's apology. "Good night," she said shakily, then made her exit from the room as fast as possible.

All the way upstairs she fiercely berated herself for having made a spectacle of her private grief in front of a group of strangers who couldn't care about her or her life.

Except for Leith.

He cared.

But he shouldn't.

He had Danica.

Whom he was going to marry.

CHAPTER NINE

AMY FELL ASLEEP almost immediately. Suzanne sat beside her for a long time, not really keeping a watch over the little girl. She didn't have to. For this first night she was sharing Amy's bedroom in case the child woke in darkness and needed reassurance. No-one wanted to risk another traumatic reaction at this early stage.

Suzanne knew the sensible thing to do was go to bed herself, but somehow she couldn't summon the will to move. It was easier to watch the moonlight filtering through the curtains and not think at all.

A light tap on the bedroom door jolted her mind into action.

Leith? Not likely, she mocked herself. Danica was not about to let him leave her side. On the other hand, it could be both of them together, come to check on Amy. Suzanne shuddered at the thought.

The light tap came again.

Ignore it, Suzanne decided savagely. Whoever it was couldn't know she wasn't asleep. She had given enough of herself to the Carew family today. The least they could do was leave her in peace for the night. Not that there was any peace for her. She was an emotional mess, torn between her memories of Brendan and the strong attraction she felt to a man who had no business in her life.

There was the slight squeak of a knob turning. Tension bit along her nerves as the door opened. Her relief was intense when the dimmed light in the hallway outlined the figure of Madeleine Carew.

"I'm sorry. Am I intruding?" she asked in a soft whisper. "I brought a thermos of hot chocolate in case you had trouble sleeping."

It was a kind thought. Before Suzanne could bring herself to move, Madeleine stepped into the room and closed the door behind her.

"I'll put it on your bedside table."

"Thank you," Suzanne murmured.

But Madeleine didn't come and go. Having put the thermos down, she moved across the room to look at Amy. "You've worked wonders with her. She looks so peaceful. At home." She reached out and gently stroked Amy's hair. "I had a little girl once."

"I know. Your husband said. It must have been terrible for you when she was taken from you."

"I think of her at night. Where she is. What she's done with her life. And all the if onlys."

As she herself wondered about her mother, Suzanne thought, except she couldn't remember her mother. It must be a lot worse for Madeleine, with remembering her daughter.

The older woman sighed, withdrew her hand and looked at Suzanne with an expression of infinite sadness. "I guess you've been thinking of your husband. It hurts for a long time when you lose someone you love. I'm sorry it was brought back to you like that tonight."

"My own fault. I should have said something before," Suzanne demurred, not wanting to talk about what had happened.

"Life does move on." It was said with soft sympathy. "It's hard to accept, but it does. Leith thinks..." Again she sighed. "He's wrong. No child can replace the daughter I had. Amy is very dear to me, but she's someone else. No-one can ever be the same."

"That's true."

It was a truth that lightened some of the burden on Suzanne's soul. Whatever the feeling between her and Leith, it was entirely different to what she had felt with Brendan. That didn't make it wrong. It simply wasn't the same. Not that it mattered. The feeling couldn't be pursued anyway. Circumstances forbade it.

"Good night, my dear," Madeleine said with caring kindness. "Try to get some sleep."

"Thank you."

In an oddly moving gesture, Madeleine touched Suzanne's hair before turning away and leaving the room. It stirred a heart-twisting need for her own family.

She rose to her feet, remembering that she hadn't called Tom. But if she called him now, he would know she was in distress. He would worry about her and there was nothing he could do, nothing of any real consequence. Better to leave the call until tomorrow. Maybe she would be more composed after a good night's sleep.

Sleep, however, proved hopelessly elusive. The hot chocolate didn't help. The unfamiliar single bed didn't help. And the moonlight didn't help. Midnight came and went. The muscles in her legs started twitching out of sheer exhaustion. It drove Suzanne out of bed. She paced the floor for a while then was tempted by the French doors, which opened onto the veranda.

Would it hurt to leave Amy for a few minutes? The child was fast asleep and looked likely to remain so. If she woke and called out, Suzanne assured herself she would hear her in the still silence of the night. She put on her silk housecoat against the coolness of the outside air, then quietly made her exit to the veranda.

Her intention to walk around was forgotten as the moonlit view of the vast vineyards drew her to the railing. What would it feel like to own all this, she wondered, her gaze sliding over the countless rows of vines marching up the far hillside, then casting back to the artistry of the formally laid out grounds and gardens closer to the house. It took generations to build up such a place. It had history and traditions behind it.

In years to come Amy would undoubtedly take great pride in it and forget all about her time in the desert with the old aboriginal woman. Forget me, too, Suzanne thought with a twinge of sadness. But as Madeleine said, life did move on. There was never any going back.

A loud creak spun Suzanne's head around to identify the sound. A figure rose from a cane armchair farther along the veranda. Her heart leapt as she recognised Leith coming towards her. He appeared to be wearing nothing but a bathrobe. Conscious of her thin housecoat covering a thinner nightdress, Suzanne's sense of propriety urged her to retreat to the bedroom she shared with Amy.

"Please wait!"

The urgent whisper halted her in mid-step.

"What do you want?" she asked.

"You must feel so alone. I didn't realise your circumstances had changed, Suzanne. Or that I, and my family, are intruding on what must be a bad time for you."

His compassion scraped over the raw needs he was in no position to answer. "It would have been better if I'd never seen you again," she said tonelessly, feeling totally bereft of any hope for the future.

"*I* make it worse?" His eyes searched hers, keenly probing for the secrets of her soul.

She turned her head aside, unwilling to let him see how deeply he affected her. She stared at the long shadows of the trees on the lawns below. Leith Carew had cast a long shadow over the last year of her marriage. Now he was so close, flesh and blood close, heart-poundingly close, yet still untouchable.

"We didn't have the child Brendan and I wanted," she blurted out, desperately trying to put some mental distance between them. "I miscarried at three months."

"I'm sorry."

He emanated a dangerously tempting warmth, a comforting warmth that she was drawn to. Why did he have to be out here with her? Why wasn't he with Danica whom he was supposed to love?

"I never knew if it was a boy or a girl," she plunged on, struggling to keep herself apart from him.

"Suzanne . . ." It was a caress on her heart.

"It's probably my fault Amy is so dependent on me," she berated herself. "It was all too easy to love her."

"And for her to love you."

The deep throb of emotion in his voice was her undoing. A moan of despair escaped her lips. She turned anguished eyes to Leith.

"But don't you see? I'm worse than Madeleine. And you're wrong about your stepmother. She doesn't confuse Amy with her lost daughter. She cares. That's all. Whereas I... I've got to leave here, Leith. It's no good."

"Suzanne, I might be wrong about many things, but—" He dragged in a deep breath. His eyes burned into hers. "When you looked at me in the Land Rover this morning, was I wrong to think what I did? That if I reached out to you..."

His hand lifted, his fingers feathering slowly up her cheek. Before she knew what she was doing she had leaned her face into his palm, blindly seeking the warmth of his skin against hers.

A deep groan issued from his throat. She jerked away from his touch. Startled guilty eyes flew to his in wild apology for the mad transgression. But it was too late to stop his hand from streaking through her hair, too late to stop his arm from scooping her in to an embrace that crushed her body to his.

"Leith!" she cried in protest.

"It's true. You do want me," he breathed, then dazed her beyond any reply by pouring a passionate rain of kisses over her hair. His hands ran feverishly over the curves of her back, revelling in the touch of her, the feel of her, wanting with an urgency that left Suzanne weak and tremulous with the same wanting.

"I couldn't sleep for thinking of you." His hand thrust through her hair again, tilting her head back. His eyes were ablaze with a wild, feverish fire. "The why or how of it doesn't matter. We were meant to come together, Suzanne."

"You mustn't . . ."

"No—" his lips grazed over hers, leaving the words in her mind stillborn "—don't say anything," he whispered, his breath as warmly seductive as his mouth. "Feel it with me. Let me show you."

His lips wove a sensual magic over hers, entrancing in their sensitivity, irresistibly persuasive in tempting her into a more intimate possession of her mouth, an unhurried gentle invasion that tantalised with tingling excitement, drawing her into a response that heightened the sensation, induced a compelling need for more.

How it suddenly became different to anything she had experienced before, Suzanne had no idea. One moment it was a kiss like any Brendan might have given her. Then she was plunged into a turbulent dimension of feeling that Leith fed with a passion she had never known. Her whole body seemed to leap in response, to pulse in wild tune to the rhythmic movement of a kiss that ravaged her knowledge of what a kiss could be.

It exploded her mind. It wakened an answering passion that rushed through her bloodstream like a dervish released from a lifetime of suppression. Her body exulted in the strength and urgency of Leith's arousal, squirming closer in yearning desire to meet its need.

When his mouth broke from hers, her fingers scrabbled through his hair to pull his head down to hers. He kissed her again. And again. His hands swept down to curve around her bottom, lift her into a more intimate fit with his body. His thighs were rock-hard against hers. His chest was a heated wall of muscle that heaved to the pressure of her breasts. She wanted him. Madly, desperately, blindly.

She felt him drag her housecoat open. A hand slid up the thin silk of her nightie to capture a breast, strong fingers gently kneading the full swell of soft flesh, exciting a sweet pleasure that craved more of his touch. His mouth left hers and trailed hot sensual kisses down her throat. She arched back, revelling in his passion for her. It was only when the cool night air wafted over her face that a thread of sanity slid into her mind.

This man was not hers to have.

No matter how incredibly right it felt, what they were doing was wrong.

"Leith—" She plucked feebly at his head. "Please . . . please, stop."

"No . . ." It was a groan of need that would not be forbidden.

"Please . . ."

"You don't mean it." He kissed his way to her face, then cupped it in his hands as his eyes seared hers with the certainty she had given him. "You

can't mean it. And I won't be turned away now that
I know."

"Danica . . ." It was all she could manage to say,
the other woman's name spilling from her lips in a
whisper of despair.

"I'll tell her. First thing tomorrow."

He said it without care, as though it was irrelevant to what was happening between them here and
now, as though nothing else mattered but the mad
whirlpool of desire that still held them in its thrall.
His hands slid down to cradle her hips, to hold her
to the intimate throb of need that denied any tomorrow, that recognised only the urgency of the
moment. His head bent, intent on taking her with
him wherever they wanted to be, regardless of time,
place or circumstance.

She almost let him. She wanted to drown in the
sensations he aroused, to forget the past and future and seize whatever they could have together.
Only at the last moment did she draw back, plac-
ing trembling fingers on his lips.

"I don't know how this happened," she cried.

"Don't think about it."

"I have to."

"No."

"You're committed to another woman, Leith."

He heaved a frustrated sigh. His eyes glittered at
her in sharp irony. "Only because I couldn't have
you."

"How can you say that?"

"It's true."

She shook her head, unable to accept it. "You hardly know me. You said Danica was the perfect match for you."

His mouth twisted, mocking his own claim. "In lots of ways she is. But none of them mean anything compared to what I feel with you, Suzanne."

"No." She dropped her hands to his chest, pushing back from the temptation he was still pressing. "This is all caught up in other things, Leith. I don't know why—"

"It doesn't matter why, Suzanne," he urged with passionate conviction. "Whatever it is, we both feel it."

"You've been with Danica so long," she argued, struggling to bring some hard reality into what was beginning to seem like sheer madness. "How can you wipe her out as though she doesn't exist any more?"

"I ache for you."

The throb of truth was in his voice, and her whole body was riven with the same ache.

"There's an empty place inside me that only you can fill, Suzanne. Not Danica."

She wanted to be filled with him, too, but she could not ignore another woman's rights. "Leith, you're messing with someone else's life. Danica Fairlie loves you. You led her to expect . . ."

"Do you want me to be honourable or honest? I'd be doing Danica a dreadful disservice if I married her now."

"How can you be so sure?"

"Because I've tasted what I can have with you. I don't want anything less."

"This . . . It's only sex."

"Is it? Let's try it and see."

It was a challenge she had no answer to. She didn't understand what she felt with Leith Carew. She only knew she had never felt it with anyone else.

"Whatever it is, it can't go on while you're tied to Danica, Leith." She remembered Danica saying she preferred honesty to people acting honourably. "If you really mean what you're saying . . ."

"I promise you I'll clear things with Danica at the first opportunity tomorrow morning."

She searched his eyes anxiously, afraid that it couldn't be as simple as that. Nothing ever was straightforward where people's emotions were concerned. "It's dreadfully unfair on Danica."

"I'll do what I can to ease the situation for her, Suzanne," he assured her.

"It seems so . . ." She shook her head as doubts flooded her mind. "What if this is all a delusion? You might be making a bad choice with me, Leith. I'm not part of your world. With Brendan . . ."

This time it was he who placed silencing fingers on her lips. "All I ask is that you let me fill the lonely space he left. Believe me, I know what I'm doing.''

His fingers trailed into her hair as he bent to graze his mouth softly over hers. "Don't worry about anything," he murmured. "I promise you it will be all right."

Her lips tingled exquisitely to the touch of his, but she forced herself to turn her face aside. "Don't start again, Leith," she whispered huskily. "I can't bear any more."

"You ache for me, too." He pressed a tender kiss on her temple. "But if you want me to wait . . ."

He left the question hanging for her to answer. Suzanne wasn't sure if it *was* a matter of waiting. She knew that this was too fast, too overwhelming for her to think straight. Perhaps physical attraction and sympathy had blown the feeling they had for each other out of all proportion. She felt too confused to say anything definite, and in the silence of the moment another voice spoke, shattering their intimate privacy.

"So this is why you didn't want to come to bed with me tonight, Leith."

Danica Fairlie's derisive taunt split Leith and Suzanne apart with the cataclysmic force of a thunderbolt.

"And Mrs. Forbes," she drawled. "What a deceitful liar you are! I almost believed you."

CHAPTER TEN

SUZANNE BURNED with guilty shame as Danica Fairlie came to a halt in front of the French doors that led to Amy's bedroom. She was hell-bent on confrontation and was leaving no room for Suzanne to escape from being included in the scene. To Suzanne's further mortification, Leith moved to place himself at her side without any deference to Danica's feelings.

"This wasn't planned, Danica," he said quietly. "I'm sorry you happened to come out here at such an inopportune moment. My intention was to tell you in the morning."

"Tell me what, Leith?" she demanded with icy disdain. "The truth that you've both evaded when I asked about your previous relationship?"

Leith shot a sharply questioning look at Suzanne before turning a frown to his fiancée. "When did you speak to Suzanne about it?"

"While we were in Alice Springs. I had a little chat with Mrs. Forbes in her kitchen." Her eyes swept Suzanne with contempt. "She lied through her teeth, insisting there had never been anything between you except official business."

"It wasn't a lie, Danica. Suzanne refused to have any personal involvement with me. Each time we met was related to the reason I was there. Ilana's death and the search for Amy."

"But you wanted her," Danica threw at him, determined on knowing all there was to know.

"Yes. I wanted her," Leith admitted without equivocation. "It was not something I went looking for. At the time, I was quite content in the relationship I had with you, Danica. I have no explanation for what I felt when I met Suzanne."

Her eyes stabbed accusingly at Suzanne. "You knew Leith wanted you. That was why you were so uneasy when I asked those questions."

"Leave Suzanne out of this," Leith cut in testily. "She's not to blame for anything."

Danica glared at him. "She's in it up to her neck. I'm not blind, Leith. She wasn't saying no to you tonight."

"I'm sorry, Miss Fairlie," Suzanne said in wretched shame. "I know there's no excuse for letting this happen. You have every right to think the worst of me."

"No, she hasn't!" Leith denied vehemently. His gaze sliced to Danica. "I wanted to know if it could be different now that Suzanne no longer has the man she loved. The opportunity presented itself and I took it. There you have it."

"Thank you, Leith," Danica said with icy satisfaction. "At last I know what I'm dealing with."

"I don't think you do," Leith said quietly. "This changes everything, Danica."

"No, it doesn't."

"If you'll let me explain . . ."

"I've got eyes in my head and a brain that can put two and two together. I don't need an explanation. She's the one woman you wanted that you didn't get, Leith. That's what this is all about."

Danica's scathing deduction jolted Suzanne. She looked at Leith in troubled uncertainty. She knew so little about him.

He was shaking his head at Danica, but with his money, power and good looks, there could be little doubt that women would make themselves available to him. Suzanne remembered his self-assurance in expecting her to fall in with his wishes when he had come to her office after seeing Brendan. He wasn't accustomed to being refused.

"You're mistaken, Danica," he said, his voice soft but carrying firm conviction. "It's much more. I have to ask you to release me from our engagement."

"You're out of your mind."

"I'll do all I can to save you embarrassment. I realise—"

"You are being ridiculous, Leith," Danica interjected. "I understand now that I should have gone to Alice Springs with you when Ilana died. No doubt the stress of such a time made your frustration over Mrs. Forbes cut more deeply than it normally would. That's why it's stuck with you so long. Plus the fact that she made herself unattainable. There's nothing more tantalising than wanting something that's unattainable."

Danica's bitter reasoning struck a raw nerve in Suzanne. She had been tormented by thoughts of what might have been with Leith Carew, making her feel guilty and disloyal to Brendan. She had fought hard to put them aside. Yet the moment that Tom had lain Amy in her arms, meeting Leith again had been uppermost in her mind. Was it simply because an attraction had been shelved, unresolved?

"It's more than that," Leith replied, a throb of passion deepening his voice.

"It's obvious you won't be content until you find out," Danica retorted.

Her eyes derisively skimmed Suzanne's disarray, the silk housecoat gaping apart, the thin nightie clinging so revealingly, its V neckline pushed aside, baring the deep cleavage of her breasts. As Suzanne reacted to the acute embarrassment of being made conscious of her state of undress, hastily trying to cover up by tying her housecoat, Danica's gaze flashed to Leith.

"So do it!" she fired at him. "Take her to bed. Get it over and done with. No doubt you'll come to your senses once the fantasy's worn off."

"For God's sake, Danica..."

"If you think I'm going to throw away our future together because you're hot for another woman, think again, Leith," she interjected fiercely. "I've put too much into it. If I have to wait a bit longer, I'll wait. But don't you tell me that what we have is over on some stupid point of honour."

However sickeningly crude her solution to the situation was, it was a brave bid to keep the man she loved, and Suzanne could not help admiring the sheer guts it took to overlook what had to be extremely humiliating. She wished she could say something to ease the terrible hurt, but having been party to the cause, however unintentionally, any word from her would be bitterly unwelcome.

Leith dragged in a deep breath and expelled it with feeling. "I know this must be a shock to you, and I appreciate how upset you are by it, Danica. I regret, very deeply, that you—"

She laughed at him, a harsh mocking sound that denied what he was saying even before she spoke. "It's no shock to me, Leith. The writing was on the wall the moment she said her husband was dead."

Her eyes glittered a wild defiance at Suzanne. "He can have you. He can have any woman he wants until the day we're married. He'll find out you're no different than the others he's had in the past. And you, Mrs. Forbes, will find out preciscly what you are to him."

She swung her gaze to Leith, her chin tilting in proud scorn of any satisfaction he might have in finally knowing what he had missed. "When you've got your mind clear of her you can come back to me. But you'd better get this clear, too. From the day that we are married, Leith Carew, you'll have no other woman but me."

It was an ultimatum that carried all the frustration and fury of a woman who had already suffered too many doubts about holding the man she was intent on marrying. Nevertheless, no matter what had gone on throughout their long relationship, Danica was still not about to give it up without a fight.

And perhaps she was right, Suzanne thought bleakly. Somewhere along the line Danica must have weighed up the pros and cons of having Leith as her husband, and she had made her decision to pursue a future with him regardless of any obstacles in her path. Suzanne was nothing more than one more obstacle to be disposed of.

Danica didn't so much as glance at her as she turned on her heel and marched off down the veranda, utterly contemptuous of what she was leaving Leith to do in her absence. Her satin-and-lace negligee billowed out behind her, a reminder that she came from the same wealthy world as the Carews, a perfect match for Leith in many ways. He had said so himself.

The slamming of the door to her bedroom punctuated her exit from a scene that had spelled out where they all were. Suzanne felt utterly wretched for having contributed to another woman's inner misery. She could not look at Leith.

"I think you should go to her," she said flatly.

"Yes. Yes, in all decency I must," he agreed, although he sounded torn by the dilemma of having to go when he wanted to stay. "I'm the one at fault," he acknowledged.

He did not make any immediate move. He heaved a deep sigh then lightly touched her shoulder. "Don't be concerned, Suzanne," he said gruffly. "I'll sort it out."

She forced herself to meet his eyes. They seemed to reflect her own anguished spirit. "We're not meant for each other, Leith. We don't match."

"I'll prove you wrong."

"Stay with Danica. No happiness comes from other people's pain."

She had known that from the beginning when she had tried her utmost to deny the attraction between them. She had sensed its potential danger, done all she could to deter him that day in the car park. For Leith to have put his marriage plans in jeopardy over her was proof enough of how disastrous any liaison between them could become. It was madness to pursue it.

"Suzanne, I've had no peace since you walked into my life. Don't deny me now. Trust me. I'll work it out."

He gave her shoulder a reassuring squeeze, then left her to go to Danica. As she watched him walk away, carrying with him an air of decisiveness, Suzanne could not help wondering if this was what it was like to be loved by him, deeply, obsessively loved, as Rolf loved Madeleine.

Was such a love wrong? Certainly Ilana and Leith had paid for it. Perhaps there was a price to pay for everything.

If she did succumb to the wild passion that had erupted between Leith and herself tonight, where would it lead? Did it have any lasting power? Did it matter? Or would it be as Danica claimed, a flash of fire quickly doused?

At the far end of the veranda, he opened the door Danica had slammed shut. If he could end his relationship with his fiancée so abruptly, he might very well have few scruples about ending any other relationship with a woman. What did she know of him apart from what he made her feel, and his single-minded devotion to his sister and her child?

You'll have to convince me, Leith, Suzanne thought with determination. Then she turned away from the sight of him entering Danica's room and slipped quickly and quietly into her own.

Amy was still sleeping peacefully, totally unaware that she had been the catalyst to destroy the peace of other people's lives.

With a sense of weary resignation, Suzanne settled herself in her bed for what was left of the night. She lay in the darkness, thinking over what Tom had said about Leith.

He dimmed the shining in you.

She knew what that meant now. Leith had taken away her inner peace, just as she had taken his. In one way Danica was right. Whatever there was between them, it needed to be resolved.

CHAPTER ELEVEN

BOTH SUZANNE AND AMY slept late. They were woken by Madeleine. She came to tell Suzanne that Tom wanted to speak to her on the telephone.

"You can take the call in my sitting room," she invited. "It's to your right along the hall. I've left the door open for you."

"Thank you." Suzanne threw her an apologetic glance as she hastily donned her housecoat. "I'm sorry you've been bothered. I should have rung Tom last night to tell him how I was getting on."

"Don't worry." Madeleine smiled. "I told your brother that Amy is responding now, but I think he wants to hear it from you."

Amy, however, was still not prepared to let Suzanne out of her sight. She tagged along to the sitting room, repeating Tom's name in happy anticipation. She did not understand how a telephone operated, and watched in puzzlement as Suzanne spoke into the receiver.

"Tom, Amy is with me. Could you speak to her?"

"Of course. But I want to speak to you, as well, Suzanne."

"In a minute," she replied. "Here's Amy."

Suzanne placed the receiver to Amy's ear, and the little girl's eyes widened when she heard Tom's voice talking to her. After her initial surprise she tried a few words back and was delighted when Tom answered her. Then she broke into giggles and handed the receiver to Suzanne.

"That sounds reassuringly normal," Tom said. "What do you think?"

"Yes, but she's hanging onto me like a security blanket. I'm hoping she'll let go a bit more today. Leith Carew's twin half-brothers have her entranced, so I'm counting on them to help."

"What about the lady who answered the phone?"

"Madeleine Carew, the twins' mother. She's very kind and caring."

"You like her." It was more a statement than a question.

"Yes. Though I don't know if Leith is going to let her have much to do with Amy. His sister appointed him guardian of her child." She sighed. "It's all rather complicated, Tom."

"Coils within coils."

Suzanne frowned, feeling a jab of disquiet at the enigmatic comment. "What do you mean by that?"

"I'm not sure." His faraway tone sent a shiver of premonition down her spine. "It's more puzzling than complicated."

Suzanne held her breath. Had Tom somehow sensed there was far more amiss here than the problem with Amy?

"I thought it must be Leith Carew," he said slowly. "But now I feel there is something about the woman and the child."

"What woman?" Suzanne asked, wondering if he meant Danica, who was to have taken the place of Amy's mother, and might still do so, for all Suzanne knew.

"The one who spoke to me."

Madeleine? Had the older woman deceived her last night? Was Leith right about his stepmother's need for Amy as a substitute for her lost daughter?

"What did she say to you, Tom?"

"It was not spoken." Then in a soft, musing voice, he added, "I had a dream. It started with you, Suzanne, and you were like a stone thrown into a pond. The ripples spread out, gathering force, spilling down a river, sweeping into a wide estuary, then far beyond, crossing oceans. Such an enormous effect from such a small action."

"It was only a dream, Tom. There's no reality to it," Suzanne said quickly, wretchedly conscious of the effect of her presence on Leith and Danica's marriage plans.

"I'd like to come and be with you."

"There's no need, Tom. I can cope," she insisted, inwardly recoiling from any well-meant interference on her behalf. Whatever was to happen with Leith, it was something she had to work through herself. It was too intensely private to share with anyone else, particularly Tom, who saw too much and knew too much.

"I know that, Suzanne," he said gently. "But I'd still like to come. I feel I can be of help."

Suzanne took a deep breath to pull herself together. She was being selfish. Amy had to be her first consideration, and Tom could help there. It was an offer she could not, in all conscience, refuse.

Besides, Danica might very well have persuaded Leith that he *had* been out of his mind last night. To jeopardise a long-planned marriage for a temporary lust, however compelling, was undoubtedly crazy. And if that was the case, Suzanne could imagine herself feeling desperate for someone of her own family to turn to and rely on for sympathetic company. Tom would be loyally steadfast in filling the role of buffer between her and the Carews.

"All right," she decided. "I'll arrange things for you. When can you get here, Tom?"

"I'll drive down. Should be there tomorrow afternoon."

"Take care."

"You, too, Suzanne."

He said it with feeling.

As Suzanne put the receiver down, her mind skimmed over all Tom had said. He seemed to have set Leith aside as a source of concern, shifting in his nebulous way to *something about the woman and the child.*

Suzanne thought it must be Amy at the centre of what Tom felt. She was there only by association, because the little girl wanted her and depended on her.

Her maternal instinct strongly aroused, she lifted the child into her arms, hugging her tightly. If Amy needed protection from warring factions in this house, Suzanne decided not to be too hasty in trying to separate herself from the situation. She would stick to Amy like glue, at least until Tom came tomorrow.

Madeleine was still in their bedroom when they returned to it. She quickly replaced a teddy bear on one of the shelves and turned to them with an overbright smile. "Would you like to have breakfast here? It's no trouble to bring it up to you."

Giving Madeleine more time to spend with Amy, Suzanne immediately thought. "Are Leith and Miss Fairlie downstairs?" she asked, inwardly cringing from having to face Danica again, but determined to do right by Amy.

Madeleine's smile barely missed turning into a grimace. "I haven't seen either of them this morning. I don't know where they are."

Suzanne wondered how long they had talked into the night. Or perhaps they had ended up doing more than talking. Her stomach cramped. "I think it's better if we come down for breakfast," she said decisively, needing to know what had happened, not only in the interests of Amy's future, but also her own.

"I'll tell Gertrude to expect you soon, then," Madeleine conceded, leaving them to dress while she arranged matters with her cook.

Amy had a stack of new clothes to choose from. Someone, most likely Madeleine, had bought a complete range of garments for a three-year-old. The little girl waited until Suzanne had dressed in light blue slacks and a white T-shirt trimmed with a garland of pink and blue flowers around the widely scooped neckline. Then she promptly eschewed the attraction of pretty dresses to select a pair of pink pants, which Suzanne had to cuff because they were slightly too long, and a white T-shirt with a spray of pink and lemon daisies.

Happily confident in her new style appearance, Amy skipped along beside Suzanne on their way downstairs, eager to explore this different world now that she was feeling more secure.

It was the kind of home that had been built on a grand scale, huge rooms with at least twelve foot high ceilings, lots of gleaming woodwork carved by master craftsmen, beautiful stained glass panels in doors and skylights, period furniture with rich furnishings to complement it, magnificent fireplaces in all the living and entertainment rooms. Everywhere one looked there was something to attract and please the eye, a figurine, a clock, a painting, a vase of beautifully arranged fresh flowers, collectors' pieces from generations of collectors.

The breakfast room was bright and cheerful, with long wide windows to invite the morning sunshine and display a view of a citrus orchard and herb garden. The floor was of glazed slate in autumn tones. A big oak table was surrounded by wooden chairs, carved in the colonial style. Since it was summer, a large copper pot filled with fresh daisies resided in the corner fireplace. The curtains were a deep yellow, as were the placemats on the table. There was a mellow warmth to the room that made it welcoming.

"Chair!" Amy cried, her eyes sparkling triumphantly as she pointed to the highchair that had been placed at the end of the long table.

Suzanne smiled at her. "Yes, your chair, Amy."

She raced off to climb into it, with Suzanne quickly following to help settle the tray in place. Jugs of fresh milk and orange juice were set ready for them, along with jars of various breakfast cereals and a platter of sliced melon sprinkled with grapes and strawberries.

"Sawberry," Amy said, pointing gleefully at the fruit the twins had incited her to try last night.

"Strawberry," Suzanne corrected her, exaggerating the consonants that she'd missed.

"Stawberry," Amy tried again.

Suzanne decided it was close enough for now. She handed one to Amy, who rolled her eyes, mimicking the twins' act as she held the fruit between her teeth and slowly bit into it. Suzanne couldn't help laughing. It set a happy tone for breakfast, and Suzanne made the most of Amy's eagerness to learn by turning the meal into a language lesson.

Gertrude brought them scrambled eggs and bacon to "help fatten the little one up." The cook, Suzanne had learnt yesterday, was a descendant of one of the German families who had first settled the Barossa Valley, and she was very proud of her heritage. She was also a big, buxom woman who was clearly of the opinion that thinness was an offence to good food.

"Eat, eat," she urged Amy, who then thought the eggs were called "eat" until Suzanne explained with gestures.

Madeleine came in at the end of the meal, a frown of puzzlement on her beautiful face. "There seems to be some alteration in Leith's plans, Mrs. Forbes. I know he intended to be here for Amy. And Danica took the week off work to be here, as well. But something must have happened either last night or early this morning because they're both gone. All Danica's things are gone, as well."

Suzanne felt a wave of intense disquiet. Had Danica insisted on going but been too upset to drive? Or had Leith gone after her, having decided he was a fool to let her go?

Reason told her there were probably a thousand explanations in between those two. Such a long and intimate relationship held too many threads of association to be sundered without repercussions. Yet reason could not stop a cold shiver running down Suzanne's spine as she remembered Tom's dream of ripples growing ever larger and gathering force enough to cross oceans.

"They didn't leave a message?" she asked, more in hope than expectation.

"No. And I haven't been able to contact either of them at any of the usual places. Nobody knows anything," Madeleine replied, clearly confused by the situation. "It's so uncharacteristic of Leith. He's always meticulously organised and—" a wry smile curved her mouth "—totally dependable."

No doubt Madeleine was well aware of Leith's opinion on his father's lack of dependability where his first family had been concerned. Suzanne made no comment, not wanting to be drawn into an involvement in family issues.

Madeleine heaved a sigh then offered an inviting smile. "Rolf suggests you might like to see over the winery." Her lustrous dark eyes warmly caressed Amy. "I'll go with you and—"

"If you don't mind, Mrs. Carew, I'd rather keep Amy close to the house today," Suzanne said firmly.

Apart from her own inclination to be at hand when and if Leith returned, she had a responsibility to look after Amy's best interests. Whatever was eventuating between Leith and Danica, and however that was going to affect her, nothing changed the fact that Amy needed to have as much time as possible with Leith, since he was taking custody of her.

Besides, Suzanne was still uneasy about Tom's remark about *the woman and the child,* and did not want to give Madeleine any more access to Amy than ordinary politeness demanded. She pondered whether to mention Tom's impending visit to Madeleine, but decided to wait and speak to Leith about it first.

"Then perhaps you'd enjoy a walk around the grounds," was Madeleine's next suggestion.

Suzanne could see no objection to that so they set off, Madeleine acting as guide and raconteur, relating when and by whom the various gardens and trees were planted. Suzanne was too distracted by thoughts of Leith and Danica to take it all in, but Amy certainly benefited by learning new names for whatever interested her.

Madeleine was only too pleased to satisfy the child's lively inquisitiveness, and Suzanne found no fault in the older woman's kindly patience. Despite her reservations, she could not help warming to Leith's stepmother. To confound Suzanne even further, Madeleine exhibited a deeper interest in her than she did in Amy, asking about her life and the family she had been adopted into.

She seemed particularly fascinated by Tom, his tribal background and how he had found Amy. Suzanne eventually felt constrained to say that Tom intended to be here tomorrow, and wanted to stay until it was time for her to leave.

"He's very welcome," Madeleine assured her warmly. "It will give us all a chance to thank him for bringing Amy back to us."

As the day wore on, Suzanne was glad she had broached the subject because Leith did not return. Not for lunch. Nor for afternoon tea.

The twins came home from school and virtually took Amy over, sweeping her off to the swimming pool where she surprised everyone by taking to the water as naturally as a fish. Her eighteen months of life in the outback had obviously taught her some of the skills of a survivor.

After a long, exciting day, Amy was more than ready for bed by seven o'clock. She dropped off to sleep almost as soon as her head hit the pillow. Suzanne had no compunction about leaving her in the bedroom by herself. Amy knew her way around the house now and had no fear of it. Suzanne switched on a dim nursery lamp so the room wasn't entirely dark should Amy wake, then went down to dinner with the family.

Whether by instruction or their own inclination, the twins had already devoured pizza and gone off to their rooms to study. This left Suzanne to dine alone with Madeleine and Rolf Carew, since Leith had still not returned.

"I must apologise on behalf of my son," Rolf said in terse disapproval. "His absence today is inexcusable. So is Danica's, for that matter. And not to leave any message..."

Madeleine touched his hand. "There must be a good reason, Rolf," she said quietly.

He was not mollified. "I intend to say a few strong words to him when he does come in, Madeleine. After what he said yesterday..." His mouth closed to a grim line and he shook his head in angry frustration with the situation.

"You are embarrassing Mrs. Forbes, Rolf," Madeleine softly chided.

He heaved an exasperated sigh and finally noticed the burning flush on Suzanne's cheeks. "I'm sorry. But it's too bad of Leith to call you in and then leave you to it, Mrs. Forbes. You can see for yourself why I think Amy would be better off with us."

"I can't give an opinion on that, Mr. Carew," Suzanne said in acute discomfort, guiltily aware that but for her, Leith and Danica would be here, demonstrating a united front.

"Mrs. Forbes was telling me about her remarkable family today, Rolf," Madeleine slid in quickly. "Fourteen adopted children."

It served to divert the conversation away from contentious issues. Suzanne did not mind talking about her brothers and sisters. She was proud of each and every one of them, their achievements, their generosity in helping others, their commitment to making the most of their lives.

It reminded her of how totally purposeless she had been since Brendan had died. No wonder Tiffany and Zachary Lee and Tom had been so concerned about her. In effect, she was letting down the family by withdrawing into herself and opting out of life. From now on, she vowed, and no matter what happened with Leith, she would go back to work and get on with living as best she could.

When she excused herself from Rolf's and Madeleine's company after dinner, that resolution was still on Suzanne's mind. She checked on Amy, found the child hadn't moved in the soundness of her sleep, then retired to the adjacent bedroom, which she had been invited to occupy.

It was, in fact, a suite designed for the private comfort and convenience of a nanny. It could be equally used as a guest suite, and Suzanne was glad it had a double bed. She was not used to the narrowness of a single bed and hoped she would sleep better tonight, although sleep was far from her thoughts at the moment.

Until Leith came back, she couldn't make up her mind about anything. Despite having a television set to watch, and a bookcase of popular novels to select from, Suzanne could not settle to passing the time in either way. Eventually she went out to the veranda and sat in the cane armchair where Leith had been last night.

She kept thinking of the things Danica had said, the tantalising nature of what was unattainable and the compulsion to satisfy an unfulfilled craving. Suzanne had no answer to what she felt for Leith Carew. It was beyond any reason or logic. In a way she wished they had never met. Leith's relationship with Danica was probably as solidly based as hers had been with Brendan. It was wrong to let this disturbing attraction interfere with it.

And yet it was there. Undeniable. Unquenchable.

The click of one of the French doors opening snapped Suzanne out of her depressing reverie. Tension whipped through her body as she saw Leith step out to the veranda. Her heart kicked into a wild gallop, trampling all sense of what was right and wrong.

He did not look her way. He walked slowly down to the set of doors that led into Amy's bedroom. He halted beside them. He lifted a hand, then hesitated about knocking, laying his palm flat against the frame instead. He shook his head wearily, dragged himself away from the doors and moved over to the veranda railing, gripping it hard as though to stop himself from following a course that he knew was highly dubious.

Suzanne felt his inner torment and could not hold herself back from him. She had caused it and it was up to her to do something about it.

The creak from the cane armchair had his head jerking towards her as she stood up. He straightened, his hands falling to his sides, clenching. He remained where he was, but Suzanne was burningly aware that he was fighting to remain still, controlling the impulse to close the distance between them. Her legs were very shaky as she walked the few metres necessary for them to be able to converse quietly.

"You wanted to talk to me?" she asked, stopping next to the veranda post nearest to him.

His eyes devoured her with a hunger that spoke of desperate need rather than desire. "I did not know what I asked of you that day in the car park when I demanded that you leave your husband for me," he said in pained remembrance. "I do know now."

"I'm sorry, Leith. If you want me to leave . . ."

"No. It's done, Suzanne. I didn't love Danica but I liked her. Very much. And she was a good friend. Reliable, sympathetic . . ." He paused to drag in a deep breath, then slowly released it. "I couldn't . . . I can't dismiss her feelings as though they mean nothing."

It was a strained plea for understanding. "What do you want to do?" she asked softly.

He gave her a cracked little smile. "It's not what I want to do, Suzanne. It's what Danica wants. And because of the position I've put her in, being virtually jilted at the altar, there's no other decent course but to respect her wishes. She deserves at least that much from me."

Suzanne looked at him in agonised uncertainty. "You don't have to keep to what you said to me last night, Leith. If it was said or done in the heat of the moment..."

"It wasn't. You know it wasn't."

The raw note of passion in his voice scraped over her inner torment. "How do we know, Leith? Maybe it is only physical attraction, and you'll start regretting what you did today. You'll end up hating me for—"

"No. Never." His eyes bleakly mocked her assertion. "Even when I wanted to hate you I couldn't. I called your strength cowardice. I bitterly condemned you for clinging to the security of a marriage that, from my own selfish viewpoint, had to be wrong. Yet all the time I was eaten up with envy for the man you loved. If I can be that man now..."

His hands unclenched, reached out in appeal. "I want to be that man, Suzanne."

She started to tremble from the sheer force of his wanting. "I don't know, Leith. You tug at me so strongly. I don't understand it. And I can't bear to have your life and Danica's life on my conscience."

"You're not responsible for what others do, Suzanne," he argued softly.

She turned away in anguish. "Where does responsibility begin and end, Leith?"

She paced to the set of doors that led into the nanny's suite, then swung to face him, compelled to pour out her doubts and fears.

"I'd rather we did what Danica suggested last night. Go to bed together. Now. Tonight. Then if it doesn't mean that much, it's not too late for you to get Danica back."

He stared at her with haunted eyes. "I've dreamed of how it might be with you for so long, Suzanne," he said, his voice furred with the torment of those dreams. "But not as a test of our feelings. As a consummation of the joy in life we can have together."

He walked towards her, his hands gesturing eloquently for her understanding. "It's not something just for me. I want it to be right for you, too. Nothing in my whole life has meant as much as this. That's my dream. And I want it to come true."

"Then play it out now!" she cried with all the urgent desperation for a resolution to what had started so long ago. "Let us both know once and for all if it's more than a dream."

With a savage motion she turned and opened one of the doors, then stood with her back to him, shaking at the moment of decision. "I'm in here tonight. Alone. I want you to join me, Leith."

CHAPTER TWELVE

SUZANNE DIDN'T WAIT for any response from Leith. She stepped inside the room, forcing a decision from him. Men were the romantics, she thought in bitter tumult. It was up to women to make the hard decisions in relationships, the practical, down-to-earth decisions. As Danica had last night.

I'm keeping faith with you, Danica. Woman to woman. Let the truth come out! Dream or reality?

The click of the door shutting behind her was the sound of decision, one way or the other. The touch of Leith's hands curling gently around the curve of her shoulders wiped all thought of Danica from Suzanne's mind.

What had she invited?

She had never been with any man but Brendan!

She quivered with apprehension—or was it excitement—as Leith's hands slowly trailed down her arms to her hands. Was she doing the right thing? Should she change her mind? Leith had built a dream around her that she wasn't at all sure she could live up to. But wasn't that what they both had to find out?

His fingers laced through hers, gripped with warm strength. He lifted her arms with his, wrapping them around her waist as he gently drew her against the solidity of his body.

She felt his cheek rub against her hair with such tender yearning that the taunting dilemma of the unknown suddenly melted away. She had to know, wanted to know everything there was to know about this man who touched her so deeply. Instinctively she relaxed, letting her mind roam free to listen to her heart.

Someone to lean on, it said. Someone who would protect her, take care of her, comfort her, love her. No harm would come to her within the warm circle of these enveloping arms and the living, breathing wall of the man behind her. It was a safe haven. The sense of belonging it gave her was sweet and soothing. But maybe that was her dream.

"It feels so good to hold you," Leith murmured. "Tell me it feels good to you, too."

"Yes," she whispered.

A tremulous sigh of pleasure rippled through him. It started an echoing tremor in Suzanne.

Then with a certainty that pulsed into her heart, he said, "This is the time for us," and she remembered his arrogant prediction on the first day they had met. *The hour will come when it is right.* But there was no arrogance in his voice tonight. It throbbed with a sense of destiny finally reaching its inevitable end. Or its real starting point.

She turned to face him, to meet him again, to welcome the sense of coming together without any cause for guilt. To the best of her ability, she had fulfilled the vows of marriage she had made to Brendan, and that was now past. Danica had released Leith from his commitment to her. There were no barriers to the full expression of what had simmered in the depths of their souls for so long. It gave Suzanne an exquisite sense of relief to at last surrender to a definite course for resolving all she had felt for him.

She moved her hands to the topmost fastening of his shirt, and with slow deliberation began the unbuttoning that would lay his chest bare to her touch. She heard his swift intake of breath, felt the tightening of his skin as his lungs expanded. Her eyes flicked up to his and were caught by the raw blaze of need in them.

"You can't know what it feels like to be with you at last, Suzanne," he said in a voice that shook with far more than relief. "When I watched you with Amy yesterday morning, there was such a glow of love shining from you, I knew it would draw Amy out of her darkness. I could barely drag myself away from it."

Her heart skipped a beat as she remembered Tom's words about Leith's darkness.

"You are so beautiful. Inside and out," he went on. "You light up a different world for me."

Suzanne had the uneasy feeling that Leith was loading too much on her, expecting too much. Her fingers faltered in their task as she worried about where this was leading.

Leith had no such hesitation in his mind or heart. He slowly gathered up the soft fabric of her T-shirt, lifted it over her head, drew it from her arms. She shivered a little as he took off her bra, exposing the full womanliness of her breasts to his gaze and touch. It was too late to back off now, she thought wildly. She had to go with her decision wherever it led.

"So very beautiful," he murmured, content to look at her as he discarded his shirt.

Suzanne stared at the strongly delineated muscles he revealed. He was far more aggressively masculine in physique than Brendan. Not that bodies mattered, she told herself, but she felt a stirring of excitement at the sheer male beauty of him. Seeing him like this, she had no difficulty in believing there would be many women willing to go to bed with him, simply for the experience.

He stripped off the rest of his clothes with a deft speed that prompted Suzanne into doing the same. Amazingly, she did not feel nervous about being completely naked in front of him. She had the confidence of knowing that he would not compare her to the other women he had known. To Leith she was special. Her body was irrelevant. Yet she felt a primitive thrill of pleasure when she saw how strongly the sight of her excited him. Or perhaps it was the thought of her.

"This was how I imagined you to be," he said huskily. "The perfect woman."

A self-conscious little laugh gurgled from her throat. "I'm not perfect, Leith."

"You are to me, Suzanne."

And the way he looked at her made her feel so infinitely desirable that she did not quibble further. Her lungs seemed to need more air than she could breathe in. Her heart started to slam around her chest in a wildly haphazard fashion. She couldn't stand the suspense of waiting a moment longer. She stepped forward, her body meeting the vibrant power of his as she flung her arms around his neck.

The effect of full, naked contact was electric. Her flesh quivered with a hot flood of sensitivity. Leith arched back in a spasm of shock, his body as taut as a bow until his breath gushed out and he gathered her to him in a fierce surge of passion, imprinting her body on his with a wild possessiveness that craved every dimension of intimacy.

"Suzanne..." It was a groan of need exploding from his lips as his head bent to hers. He claimed her mouth with such deep, ravaging hunger that she could feel it drawing on her stomach, her thighs, stirring a sensation of weak emptiness that yearned to be filled by him.

Never before had she felt such a compelling need for instant gratification. All her previous experience was of soft, caring foreplay until she was ready to enjoy the pleasure of coming together. But with Leith it was unbelievably different. She felt as though she was dying to have him inside her, to feel his strength feeding her hunger, giving back what he seemed to be taking with such devouring intensity.

She wrenched her mouth from his, wondering if she was mad but uncaring of any consequences. "I want you now, Leith," she said, hardly believing she could utter such brazen words, but he believed them.

He swept her onto the bed with him without a moment's hesitation, meeting the urgency of her desire with a thrust so hard and deep that her body arched convulsively at the exquisite shock of his invasion. It was like thunder rolling through her, thunder and lightning as he struck again, a driving bolt of sensation that was ecstatically satisfying.

"Yes, yes," she cried in a frenzy of excitement, her hands urging him into a pounding rhythm that swelled and retreated in a tantalising dance of quivering anticipation and shuddering fulfilment. Such sweet agony and ecstasy, her whole body tingling with expectation, flooding with tidal waves of exultant pleasure, floating on an ocean of it as Leith spilled himself inside her and carried her with him to lie cradled in his arms, ensuring the sweet lingering on of their union.

Her muscles convulsed around him with the sheer joy of remembrance of how it had been, loving the feel of him, not wanting to release him, intensely possessive in holding him within her. She felt him stir and grow hard again, filling her with the promise of more.

"I can't have enough of you, Suzanne," he breathed through her tumbled hair.

He rolled onto his back, lifting her on top of him, propping her there with his powerful thighs. She leaned forward, sliding her hands over the heaving sweat-slickened muscles of his chest. He stroked her back, clawed it erotically with the fine edge of his fingernails. As she shuddered in pleasure he pulled her forward to capture the taut peak of one of her breasts in his mouth, drawing on it with such deep intensity that it sent piercing shafts of sensation down to her loins.

He raised his hips, driving himself fully inside her as he moved his mouth from one breast to the other, taking in her flesh as he gave his, maintaining a rhythm that drove Suzanne completely mindless. Her body reacted with wanton wildness, threshing over his, savouring, relishing, insanely greedy for the tumultuous beat of escalating sensitivity. There came a moment when she felt as though every cell in her body was melding into some other life form. She felt Leith shudder beneath her and knew it was the same for him, for both of them together.

Then she was lying on her back and he was leaning over her, kissing her with soft, tender sensuality, soothing her tremors with gentle caresses, pouring out passionate words of love. She could barely lift a hand to his face. She felt as though she was swimming slowly up through a whirlpool. She had difficulty in focussing her eyes on his. Her fingertips found his lips.

"Leith," she whispered on a breath of incredulous wonderment, then gasped as his mouth opened and closed on her fingers, his eyes still blazing with desire for her. "It's not a dream?" she asked dazedly.

He released her fingers, kissed her palm, her wrist, the inside of her elbow. Her sluggish pulse leapt into a faster beat.

He smiled. "If it's a dream, Suzanne, I never want to wake from it." He pressed her hand over his heart. "Is that real enough for you?"

His strong life force pulsed through her skin, linking her to him as surely as all that had gone before. "It's never been like this for me," she confessed.

"Nor for me."

Perhaps it was crazy to believe him, but she did. Despite whatever number of women there had been in his past, she believed that they were as nothing compared to what she and Leith had known together this night. It couldn't be any other way. Yet what did it mean? Did it have any meaning at all beyond the ecstatic pleasure they had given to each other?

"So where does this leave us now?" she asked.

He grazed his lips over hers with teasing sensuality. "Very much in love," he murmured.

She shook her head. Could it be as easy as that? To simply accept they were meant to come together and everything else would somehow sort itself out? As stunned as she still was by what she felt with Leith, Suzanne was wary of taking anything for granted in such a strange set of circumstances.

"I meant where does that leave us practically, Leith?"

A rueful expression flitted over his face. "Well, I promised Danica a few things. I thought they were reasonable requests, but they do propose some difficulties for us."

"Such as?"

She couldn't resist running her hand over his chest and playing with the sprinkle of silky golden curls that arrowed down from the base of his throat. It was a heady intoxicant, having the freedom to touch him however she liked. It was several moments before she realised that Leith hadn't answered her. Her eyes lifted to his in questioning appeal. She found him smiling at her, his eyes glowing with blissful pleasure.

"The difficulties," she reminded him, unable to stop herself from smiling at her pleasure in him.

"That we make no public announcement for six months," he replied, confidently assuming they would have an announcement to make. "It's a matter of pride. Danica didn't want it to be seen that I went from her to you at a moment's notice."

"And the other conditions?"

"Apply only to me. Discretion with mutual social acquaintances. The disposal of various gifts. Business matters." His eyes probed hers, wanting to see the same confidence he had in their future together. "Can you handle that, Suzanne? Six months of waiting?"

"It does ensure we're not rushing into something that might be a mistake, Leith," she said slowly, wondering if Danica had figured on that when she had stipulated no public announcement. Was she still counting on getting Leith back?

"It's no mistake," Leith said with conviction, and the burning look in his eyes was intent on searing away any doubts she might have. "We were meant for each other, Suzanne."

He kissed her with a passion that recognised no limit to the desire that stirred between them. Suzanne dizzily acknowledged that she couldn't have enough of him, either. If she lit up a different world for Leith, he certainly did the same for her, drawing her into a world of feeling she had never known, a world where all her senses were more intensely alive.

She did things she had never done before, revelling in exploring the sensuality Leith aroused in her and totally enthralled with his response to any initiative she took. Nothing she did was wrong. Everything was deliciously right, intoxicatingly right, beautifully right.

Would it last six months? she wondered in the hazy dream world of total satiation. Would it go on forever? Then, on the furry edge of sleep, another thought slid into her mind.

"Leith?"

"Mm?"

"There's one small problem that everyone seems to have forgotten."

"What's that?"

"Amy. What's going to happen with Amy?"

Leith's hand swept slowly down Suzanne's back. His arm tightened around her. "To Amy, you're her mother already, Suzanne."

"But the six months?"

"We'll work something out. If Amy knows what's at the end of it, she'll be happy enough to wait. Don't worry about it."

But Suzanne couldn't help worrying. She could hardly stay in the Carew home for six months if Danica's conditions were to be adhered to. That meant leaving Amy with Rolf and Madeleine, since Leith could not be with her all the time. It would be impossible for him to neglect his business for six months. But would Amy be all right with Madeleine?

Then Suzanne remembered that Tom was coming tomorrow. Tom would know, she thought on a wave of relief. He had felt that she needed his help and he was right. She smiled as she relaxed and invited sleep again. Tom might know too much, but she was glad he was her brother. And he was coming tomorrow.

CHAPTER THIRTEEN

MADELEINE AND ROLF were seated at the breakfast table when Leith and Suzanne came downstairs with Amy the next morning. Rolf glowered at his son, although he made an effort to greet Amy with grandfatherly indulgence and Suzanne with warm hospitality. In her quiet, charming manner, Madeleine asked what they'd all like for breakfast and went off to tell Gertrude.

"We missed you and Danica yesterday," Rolf directed at Leith as soon as they were seated. "Is there some problem?"

"Danica is no longer my fiancée," Leith answered coolly. "Though in deference to her wishes, that is a private announcement, not a public one, so please keep it private."

Rolf frowned at him, then shot a probing look at Suzanne before returning a speculative gaze to his son. "Well, I hope you know what you're doing. You've got Amy to consider. Or has that changed, as well?"

Leith surprised his father by breaking into a broad smile. "I have Amy's best interests at heart. You have no cause for concern about that."

Rolf raised his eyebrows. "I suppose it's too much to ask how you intend to deal with these best interests, now that you're not getting married?"

"I'll work it out." Leith turned his smile to Suzanne. "And I have the best possible person to work it out with."

Rolf swung his gaze to Suzanne assessingly. She fought to keep a warm tide of blood from sweeping up her neck but knew she hadn't succeeded when her cheeks started to burn. Rolf couldn't know that Leith had spent most of the night in her bed, only leaving at dawn in case Amy should walk in on them. However, it was unlikely he had forgotten the way Leith had reacted at the dinner table when she had said her husband was dead.

"I see," he muttered. Then he turned an ironic smile to his son. "Never thought Danica was right for you, anyway."

Suzanne wished she could ask why not, but did not want to draw more attention to herself at this uncertain juncture.

Madeleine returned to the breakfast room, and Rolf's attention instantly switched to her. "Leith has broken his engagement to Danica, Madeleine. But this remarkable piece of news is to be kept under wraps until further notice," he announced with surprisingly good humour.

She looked sharply at Leith. "Didn't she want Amy?"

Her mind had winged instantly to the child, Suzanne noted, increasing her concern about leaving Amy in Madeleine's care. She hoped Tom would be able to sort the truth out for her.

"Amy had nothing to do with it," Leith answered briefly.

"But what are you going to do about Amy now?" Madeleine persisted.

Leith smiled at her. "Well, today Suzanne and I are going to take her out for a picnic lunch. We'll be home before Suzanne's brother arrives this afternoon."

His warm use of her first name was in such obvious contrast to the distant formality of Mrs. Forbes, it swung Madeleine's gaze to Suzanne, her dark eyes widening as her mind clicked through the same speculation that had sped through Rolf's.

"That will be nice," she said limply. "It looks like being a beautiful day for a picnic. I'll tell Gertrude to prepare a basket, shall I?"

"No. We'll stop somewhere and buy something, thanks, Madeleine," Leith answered easily.

They all made a point of giving Amy most of their attention throughout breakfast. Nevertheless, Suzanne was extremely conscious of Madeleine and Rolf taking note of Leith's manner towards her, the warm pleasure in her company that he did nothing to disguise.

There was no reason he should hide it, Suzanne told herself, yet she felt uncomfortable about the conclusions that were clearly being drawn. It was too soon. What if their relationship didn't stand up to the pressures and expectations of everyday life? She knew nothing about Leith's business, for a start. Not like with Brendan. And what about his social world? Was she capable of fitting in with what he would want of her?

It was much later in the day that Suzanne began to doubt that any of that mattered. Leith was so happy to be with her and Amy. And she felt happy, too. Happier than she ever remembered.

They had a simple picnic of hamburgers and chips and chocolate milkshakes in a children's park. Amy was beside herself with gleeful excitement when Leith showed her how a swing worked and helped her slide down a slippery dip. They laughed together, held hands, felt like a family, and all the time Leith's eyes kept telling Suzanne that this was what he wanted. More than anything else in the world.

Tom must have made good time on his long trip down from Alice Springs. When they returned to the house his Safari van was in the driveway and he was being greeted by Madeleine at the front door. The moment Leith had brought the Land Rover to a halt at the foot of the steps, Suzanne was out and gathering Amy into her arms to race up and greet her brother. Leith was not slow to follow her.

Tom and Madeleine moved to meet them. Tom was not given to smiles, yet as he watched the three of them mount the steps, his face slowly broke into a grin of rare pleasure.

"I didn't expect you so early!" Suzanne cried, her heart lifting at this evidence of Tom's benevolent approval at what he saw.

"It became a lighter journey on the way," he replied, his dark eyes shining from her to Leith and back to her. "It is a bright day, is it not?"

She laughed. Nothing could stay hidden from this unique brother of hers. "Yes. I believe it is, Tom."

"I am glad it is so." He turned to Leith and offered his hand. "For my sister," he said with all the dignity of a tribal elder giving his blessing.

"It's good of you to come," Leith said warmly, not understanding the significance of Tom's words or gesture but pleased to welcome the man who had found Amy.

The little girl decided it was time for her to claim Tom's attention and she broke into an excited clamour of indistinguishable words. Tom laughed and hoisted her onto his shoulder to her squeals of delight. Madeleine finally stepped in, assuming her role as hostess, and ushered them all inside the house.

Suzanne managed some time alone with Tom once he was shown to the room prepared for him. Madeleine withdrew, and Leith inveigled Amy downstairs with the promise of ice cream in the kitchen.

"What is it you want to tell me, Suzanne?" Tom asked as soon as they were left together.

She explained the situation as it now stood, and Tom listened with the imperturbable air that was so much a part of his character. He made no comment nor asked any questions. When she had finished relating all but the intimate details of last night, Tom slowly nodded his satisfaction.

"I did not understand before but it was Brendan who was wrong for you, Suzanne," he stated.

She made a strangled sound of protest.

He shook his head at her instinctive denial. "It was a good path, but not the best one, and you have been hurting from it for a long time. Ever since Leith Carew came into your life. I see that now. It is he who can give you the feeling of completeness that you sought by having a baby."

Suzanne stared at her brother. She had never confided her desperation at not being able to conceive quickly after her miscarriage. Had she been so transparent to him? Or did he somehow sense these things?

"How can you be so sure about Leith, Tom?" she asked, wanting her doubts about the future settled if possible. "I'm not yet sure myself," she confessed.

"There is no mistaking the shining of that kind of love, Suzanne," he replied matter-of-factly, as though there could be no question about it. "I have seen it with Tiffany and Joel. Rebel and Hugh have it, too. It was less with you and Brendan, but I thought it a quieter love. And you were content. Until he came."

"Did I do wrong by Brendan?" she asked in pained confusion over the choices she had made.

"No. He counted himself a fortunate man to have you as his wife. You gave him all he wanted of you. He was a good man, but being a doctor was most important to him. That was Brendan's passion. For Leith Carew, you are his passion."

It was an insight that struck true to Suzanne once it was spoken so bluntly. It wiped away the last lingering twinges of guilt over any disloyalty to Brendan. But where Leith was concerned, was passion enough to build a good life together?

Wasn't passion more related to lust than to love? Yet when had she known Tom to be wrong in his perceptions? And these last few hours with Amy in the park, it hadn't been desire simmering between her and Leith. It had been blissful contentment. Peace. Deep inner peace.

"Thank you, Tom," she said with heartfelt gratitude for clearing up much of her inner confusion.

He shrugged as though it was of no account. A simple fact of life.

"What do you feel about Madeleine now that you've met her?" she asked, hoping he could help solve the problem of what was best for Amy.

His brows lowered in a frown of puzzlement. "I need more time with her."

She smiled. "No time like the present. Let's join everyone downstairs."

Leith had already proposed one solution to the question of what to do with Amy. He thought it best that the little girl return to Alice Springs with Suzanne. He would fly up and visit them every weekend until the six months were up. Then, once they were married, there would be no separation for any of them.

Suzanne, however, was not convinced that was the best solution. She felt that Leith was rushing the decision to marry before any real foundation was laid for a future together. Apart from which, she was concerned about separating Amy from the rest of her family.

The little girl adored the twins. As Suzanne watched Jeb and Stuart playing with her in the swimming pool that afternoon, she could not help feeling it would be wrong to take Amy away. If Tom could sort out the problem with Madeleine, surely some better arrangement could be made.

She watched Tom converse with his hostess and wondered if he was getting any closer to defining his feeling about Madeleine. He gave no sign of it, but Tom rarely did show his thoughts. It was Madeleine who was doing most of the talking, Tom nodding, unconsciously emanating the air of age-old wisdom that seemed etched on his dark aboriginal face.

Afternoon passed into evening. Tom spent the time before dinner with Madeleine and Rolf while Suzanne and Leith settled Amy for the night. It was immediately clear what they had been talking about when Suzanne and Leith entered the lounge for a predinner drink.

"Damned police were useless," Rolf was saying. "As for the private investigators I hired . . ."

Madeleine stiffened. Rolf, whose awareness of his wife was ever-constant, swung his head around, saw Leith and clamped his mouth shut. Tom looked up from the photograph album that Madeleine had been showing him, but his gaze wasn't drawn to either Rolf or Leith.

His eyes targeted Suzanne with such a strange look that she wasn't sure he was really seeing her at all. It raised a prickle of gooseflesh on her skin. Something had clicked in his mind. She was sure of it.

Then Rolf stood up and started asking about drinks for her and Leith. Madeleine slid the album from Tom's lap, closed it and put it on a side table next to the sofa where they sat.

"Another beer for you, Tom?" Rolf asked.

He reacted slowly, as though coming out of a trance. "No. Thank you. If you don't mind I'd like to make a phone call before dinner."

"By all means. My study is across the hallway. Phone in there," Rolf invited.

There was an awkward silence as Tom left Madeleine's side to follow Rolf's directions. Suzanne could feel Leith's anger at what he guessed had been transpiring, an attempt to win Tom's sympathy for Madeleine's cause to keep Amy here with her. Suzanne was not so sure of that. She quickly excused herself to follow Tom and find out precisely what had happened.

She caught up with him in the hallway. "Tom? Is there something I should know?" she quickly asked.

He gave her an enigmatic look. "Coils within coils, Suzanne."

"Whom do you have to ring?"

He shook his head. "Go back to the others. I make them feel uneasy as it is, and I'm relying on you to smooth things over."

Suzanne knew there was no fighting Tom's decision. His sense of integrity would not be shaken, and when he made up his mind about something there was no shifting it. She had to be content to wait. Whatever he was thinking or doing, he would tell her when he was ready. She hoped desperately it would not be something that would turn her against Leith.

Leith, however, had also made up his mind, and he had no hesitation about telling Suzanne his decision later that night. He paced around her bedroom in tense agitation, words pouring out in a torrent of passion.

"Amy goes with you, Suzanne. I will not leave her here with Madeleine. God knows what sick fantasies she's nursing. Bringing out that album for Tom. It's been over twenty years and she still can't let it go."

"Did you forget Amy all those months she was lost in the desert, Leith?" Suzanne asked quietly.

"No, of course not! But I wasn't looking for Amy in the face of every child I saw in the street!" he retorted. "I tell you she's sick, Suzanne. Mentally and emotionally sick about that daughter she lost. Ilana suffered for it, and I won't have Amy suffer for it."

"How did Ilana suffer for it?"

"Madeleine used to cry over her. Ilana was only seven years old when my father brought Madeleine home with him. She hated it when Madeleine tucked her in bed at night and kissed her with tears in her eyes. We knew why." He gave a harsh laugh. "We'd already had a year of knowing why since our father had stayed in the United States, searching for Madeleine's lost daughter."

"Leith, that was a long time ago. And the loss would have still been very painful then," Suzanne pointed out. "I haven't seen Madeleine crying over Amy."

"Why do you suppose she was showing Tom the photographs if it's not on her mind all the time?"

Leith shook his head, completely out of patience with the situation. "In any event, Ilana didn't want Madeleine to have Amy."

"Leith, what happened to your mother?" Suzanne asked, wanting to know more about his life.

He frowned. "She died giving birth to Ilana. She almost died having me. She was warned not to have any more children but she wanted a daughter so she decided to take the risk."

"How old were you then?"

"Ten."

"You weren't enough for her?"

"It was her choice, Suzanne," he said curtly, dismissing any implied criticism of his mother.

It was a choice Suzanne would never have made, to risk leaving behind a motherless ten-year-old son for the possibility of having another child. Had Leith felt unloved? Abandoned?

"You must have missed her terribly," Suzanne said softly.

"I had Ilana to look after."

The big brother who took the place of both mother and father, Suzanne thought, forming a bond that probably didn't give Madeleine much of a chance of reaching them, given the circumstances of their father's second marriage. Leith and Ilana may not have been openly hostile, but they would not have been sympathetic to Madeleine's position.

Suzanne could see every side, and she couldn't feel right about rejecting Madeleine as a possible bad influence in Amy's life. She went over to Leith and slid her hands around his neck. "We don't have to decide right now, Leith," she pleaded.

She felt the tension ease out of him as he wrapped his arms around her. "I wish to hell Danica hadn't made those conditions. It would solve everything if we could get married straightaway."

Suzanne did not believe that. Having been brought up in a family where everyone helped everyone else, she was distinctly uncomfortable about walking away from problems that needed to be solved. The rifts in the Carew family would only deepen and become more embittered if she agreed to Leith's course.

However, he was in no mood to have that pointed out to him. And one thing Suzanne had learnt was there had been too much expected of Leith, and too little giving coming his way. Which was something she could start redressing right now. Other matters could be postponed until tomorrow. Or the next day. Or the next.

She pressed closer, moving her body invitingly against his, her eyes openly declaring what she wanted. "Marriage can wait," she said huskily. "But I can't. I'm dying to make love with you. I want you as completely as I had you last night."

CHAPTER FOURTEEN

DANICA ARRIVED next morning, unheralded, unexpected, wanting to see Suzanne and no-one else.

Madeleine delivered the message. She had left Danica waiting in the formal living room. It was not a social call. She had refused the offer of any refreshments. She had something to say to Suzanne, and that was the sum total of her purpose in coming.

Madeleine made a tactful withdrawal while Suzanne and Leith were absorbing the shock of this announcement.

Leith's first reaction was strongly against the meeting. "I won't have Danica abusing you for my decision, Suzanne. She had no right to speak as she did to you the other night. If she wants something, she deals with me. I'll go and talk to her."

"No. She's hurt, Leith. Seeing you would only hurt her further," Suzanne argued softly. "I think you should respect her wishes."

He frowned. "I don't like it. She has no business coming to you."

"If it answers some need in her, don't you think that's worthwhile, Leith? I didn't mean to hurt her, but I did. I want to help if I can."

His eyes softened with his feeling for her. "Your giving to others, your caring and compassion, are so much part of why I love you, Suzanne. But I doubt Danica wants that from you. And if she's come to make trouble between us..."

"Don't you trust what I feel for you, Leith?"

He searched her eyes anxiously. "I don't want Danica turning you against me. What's past is past. I swear it. All I want now is a future with you."

She held his gaze with unwavering conviction. "A good marriage is based on understanding, Leith. There shouldn't be any secrets. I promise you, if Danica says anything that gives me a problem, I'll talk it out with you. Is that assurance enough for you?"

He heaved a deep sigh, then took her hands in his and lifted them to his lips, pressing a slow, impassioned kiss on each one. "All my instincts rebel against letting you go to her," he said huskily. "Promise you'll come straight back to me."

"I promise."

She smiled to ease his perturbation, then left to go to Danica, churning inwardly over what Danica might have to say. Had she come to turn her against Leith if she could?

Suzanne couldn't help feeling extremely apprehensive as she walked down the hallway to the liv-

ing room. The door was shut. She paused a
moment to gather her composure, gave a tap on the
door to announce her arrival, then went straight in,
not wanting to give the impression that she was
daunted by this meeting in any shape or form.

Danica Fairlie stood by a set of French doors on
the other side of the room, apparently staring out
at the row of roses that edged the lawn on that side
of the house. At the sound of Suzanne's entry, she
dropped her hand from the curtain and watched it
fall into place before slowly turning around.

She was dressed to daunt any other woman. A
stylish suit in a vibrant coral linen made the most of
her tall, slim figure. Her long blond hair was wound
into an elegant chignon with a few artful strands
wisping around her ears. Pearls gleamed on her
lobes and around her throat. Her make-up was
perfect, complementing the colour of her clothes
and highlighting her lovely blue eyes.

She made Suzanne feel frumpish in her cotton
skirt and blouse, and very much aware that she
hadn't applied the slightest dash of lipstick, let
alone full make-up. But appearances were not the
issue here, unless Danica was at pains to show Suzanne that she was far more suited to Leith's world
than Suzanne was.

A sardonic smile curled the coral lips. "So you
came. I wondered if you'd have the guts to stand up
to Leith."

"You asked to see me, Miss Fairlie," Suzanne replied evenly.

"Yes. But I expected Leith would be hell-bent on protecting you," Danica mocked.

"If you want to see him instead..."

"No. Leith and I have no more to say to each other." Her eyes glittered with hard determination. "I've decided I don't want him back, regardless of what happens with you and him."

She strolled forward and propped herself on the widely cushioned armrest of a chesterfield sofa. "I've been through that once because of you, Mrs. Forbes," she said derisively. "And I don't care to try it twice."

Suzanne frowned. "I don't understand what you're referring to."

"No?" Her eyebrows lifted. "Leith hasn't told you how he reacted to your rejection of him the first time around?"

"He hasn't spoken of it to me," Suzanne replied quietly, recalling that Danica had spoken of deep bitterness in their last tete-a-tete.

"Well, the first thing he did when he came home from Alice Springs was to break off with me. Total withdrawal. He changed from being a social animal into a curt beast who'd have no truck with anyone. After six months of that he changed again, partying like there was no tomorrow and going through a string of women who never lasted more than one night in his bed."

She paused to give Suzanne a grim little smile. "When he finally came back to me, he gave me to understand that he'd come to his senses and that I was the woman he wanted in his life."

"When was that?" Suzanne asked, stunned by the deep and violent effect she had had on Leith's emotions and actions.

"Well, this is a nice little piece of irony for you," Danica drawled. "By your count it was a week before your husband died, Mrs. Forbes."

Suzanne's heart contracted as though from a blow. For Leith to have gone back to Danica precisely when Brendan and she were starting their second honeymoon... Was it ironic? Or had Leith felt some sense of finality about her?

For some reason Tom's words drifted through her mind, *coils within coils.* So many strange occurrences. Why should it be Tom who found Amy and brought the child to her? And now this! What did it all mean?

"I'm sorry," Suzanne murmured, not knowing what else to say.

Danica shrugged. "I was a fool to take him back. It was never the same as before." Her mouth twisted. "And living in hope isn't exactly joy and bliss. I realise now that I'm well out of it. So I give you my blessing, Mrs. Forbes. Leith is all yours if you want him."

"I wish I could do something for you," Suzanne said sincerely.

Danica gave a brittle laugh. "You did. But for you I would have made the biggest mistake of my life. Leith might have been the best catch in Adelaide but I do happen to want a husband who loves me." Her voice hardened as she added, "So damned much he never even wants to look at another woman."

While she was in total sympathy with these sentiments, Suzanne felt that Danica would not welcome any comment on them from her. She did wonder if Danica had been more in love with the best catch than with the man himself, but she held her silence on that, as well. The other woman's pride might have voiced that remark.

Danica stood up abruptly, stiffening her spine and tilting her chin with an air of proud disdain. "I didn't come to cry on your shoulder, Mrs. Forbes. Now that I've had time to adjust my thinking, this is all behind me."

"Why did you come, Miss Fairlie?" Suzanne asked, privately thinking Danica had old scores to settle before she made her exit from Leith's life.

"I came because of Amy," was the totally surprising reply. "I don't want to make difficulties for her. The poor little kid has had a hard enough time as it is. In spite of the fact that she did not come to me naturally, I did feel for her. And I would have tried to be a good mother to her."

Spots of hot colour ruined the subtle effect of the blusher Danica had used, but did not for one moment lessen her dignity as she spelled out her main purpose. "I'm not so selfish that I'd put my pride ahead of her welfare. I've reconsidered what I demanded of Leith. At the time, I wasn't thinking of Amy. For her sake, I withdraw all objection to you and Leith doing whatever you want, whenever you want."

Suzanne felt ashamed for thinking at all meanly of this woman. Underneath the hard protective shell she had adopted today, she had a good heart. "Thank you, Miss Fairlie," she said in true admiration for a generosity of spirit that few people would have in this situation.

Danica gave her a wry smile. "I'm indulging myself by being noble and honourable. I wouldn't want you to think you're the only one who can do it, Mrs. Forbes."

Suzanne shook her head. "I think, in other circumstances, you and I could have been very good friends."

"I doubt it. I'm far too strong-willed for you to be comfortable with me."

Suzanne disagreed but there was no point in arguing about it. She knew her will was every bit as strong as Danica's, although the choices they made were probably based on different priorities. That didn't stop Suzanne from admiring and respecting the other woman's inner strength.

Danica apparently interpreted her silence as weakness. She cocked her head slightly, running coldly assessing eyes over Suzanne. "I wonder what Leith sees in you that he couldn't find in me."

Suzanne remained silent. She did not want to add insult to injury, and Danica would surely bristle in offence at anything she said.

The other woman let out a peeved sigh and walked to the French doors where she had been standing earlier. She swept the curtain aside once more and stared out.

"It cuts me to the quick to know that this place will never be mine now," she said, the bitter frustration of thwarted ambition edging her voice. "It's beautiful as it is, but I could have turned it into a showcase that would have been the envy of everyone who came here. And I would have been the perfect hostess for it."

Suzanne was stirred to comment this time. "I'm sorry, Danica. But if you want me to be honest, I doubt that means much to Leith."

She dropped the curtain and swung around, her eyes glittering with all the ferocity of a woman scorned. "Then I'll be just as honest back. And it's the only thing out of all of this that gives me any satisfaction whatsoever, because it's the most perfect piece of female bitchery."

Her mouth took on a sneer as she walked towards Suzanne. "As a dyed-in-the-wool goody-two-shoes, you'll undoubtedly hold Leith off until you're married. Well, let me tell you that come the wedding night, you'll find out one thing for certain. He's not much of a lover."

She paused in front of Suzanne, her eyes glittering with savage mockery. "And when you lie in his bed afterwards, feeling let down and disappointed, you can remember I told you so."

She flashed her teeth in a travesty of a smile, stepped past Suzanne and made her exit from the living room on what she considered the ultimate punch line, closing the door behind her with a decisive click.

Suzanne hoped it did give Danica some sense of satisfaction, for as far as she was concerned, the *honest* shot only served to emphasise that Danica had not been the right woman for Leith, and never would have been.

A wave of sadness swept through Suzanne as she thought how different the past eighteen months might have been if she had allowed herself to listen to Leith that day in the car park, if they had come together then. She could not blame Leith for what he had done in trying to forget her. She had been just as desperate to get him out of her mind, as driven about having a baby as he was in going from woman to woman.

Brendan might still be alive today if she had left him when Leith had asked her to. Danica would not have been so badly hurt. Was honour better than honesty?

Yet even now, knowing all she did, Suzanne knew in her heart that she could not have broken the vows she had made to Brendan.

And what about Amy? Would the little girl have ever been found if there had been a different sequence of events?

Who was to say what was best? There was no changing what had been done, anyway. And Leith was waiting for her, waiting to hear that nothing would stop them from having a future together. There was no longer any embargo on when they could marry. Danica had cleared the path for them.

CHAPTER FIFTEEN

SUZANNE DID NOT tell Leith everything Danica had said to her. She did not want to diminish the other woman in Leith's eyes, and the freedom Danica had given them more than made up for the injury she might have done if Suzanne had not known better.

For the rest of the day they were in a state of euphoric happiness, talking over plans that would best suit the new situation. They took Amy for a walk through the family vineyards, ending up at the winery since Suzanne insisted they both needed to know something of the family business. Leith gave them the full tour through the winemaking process and spoke of sales figures that were astronomical to Suzanne.

"You really love everything about this, don't you?" she remarked, hearing the enthusiasm and satisfaction in his voice.

It gave him pause for thought. "It's what I know. What I was brought up to do. It's second nature to me." He gave her a wry grimace. "Though to tell you the truth, it hasn't meant anything to me these last eighteen months. It kept me occupied. That's all. Sharing it with you makes it meaningful again.''

Her eyes sparkled with joy. ''Well, it might take me a while to learn, but I want you to always share it with me, Leith.''

''What about you, Suzanne? Do you want to continue nursing?''

She smiled. ''Not for a while. I'd really like to have a family.''

He grinned. ''I'll do my best. But if you'd like to go back to work, that's fine by me, too. More than anything, I want you to be happy with me.''

She laughed. ''Right now, I couldn't be happier.''

''Nor me.''

They decided to announce their marriage plans that evening, thereby settling the question of Amy's future welfare once and for all. There was no longer any concern in Suzanne's mind that the decision to marry was premature or unsound. Whether it had been some instinctive recognition of each other or some other intuitive force, she did not know, but the feeling of strong connection that had sprung between them at their first meeting had been reinforced a hundredfold in the past few days. Life without Leith had become unimaginable.

When they went downstairs after settling Amy for the night, Suzanne was disappointed to find that Tom hadn't yet returned from his day in Adelaide. He had set out early this morning, before Suzanne was out of bed. What on earth he was doing in the city, she had no idea. He had simply left a message that he had gone and would be back this evening.

She had a brief moment of disquiet as she and Leith entered the room where Madeleine and Rolf were relaxing with a pre-dinner drink. She hoped the older couple would accept the news gracefully and accept her into the family without too many reservations. Not that it would change her mind, but she wanted everyone to be happy.

Rolf rose to his feet to offer drinks but Leith forestalled him, wasting no time in making his announcement. "Champagne tonight! I want to celebrate the best day of my life. Suzanne has agreed to marry me."

"Ah!" said Rolf, nodding satisfaction. Then with an oddly tentative smile, his eyes searching for a rapport in the eyes that were so like his, he said, "You are my son, Leith, and I want you to be happy. It was fairly evident that some portentous change was taking place these past few days. I hope you've found the woman of your dreams as I did with Madeleine."

He turned to Suzanne. "It's not for me or Madeleine to pass judgment, but we are very favourably impressed by the quiet steadiness you have brought into this household. We couldn't supply whatever it was Leith needed after Ilana's death. Neither did Danica. But something shines from you that all of us respond to. Especially Amy."

"Yes," Madeleine agreed softly, rising from her chair. Warmth glowed in her eyes as she came forward to take Suzanne's hands and press a welcoming kiss on her cheek. "We hope you'll be very happy together," she said with such genuine sincerity that it was impossible to doubt it.

"Thank you," Suzanne murmured, deeply touched by the older woman's graciousness.

Rolf joined his wife and kissed Suzanne's other cheek. Then he gave Leith's hand a vigorous shake.

"You don't mind about Amy being with us?" Suzanne couldn't stop herself from asking Madeleine.

"You love her, too," Madeleine answered. "There's no question that she'll be happy with you and Leith, Suzanne."

Which put an entirely new perspective on what had been happening. It was Leith's proposed marriage to Danica that had caused the dissent over Amy, not Madeleine's hankering for a daughter. Or so it now seemed.

Whatever the truth of it, Rolf had no compunction in breaking open his finest bottle of champagne and pouring out his approval of this latest development in his family's affairs. He was proposing a toast to future happiness when Tom walked in, carrying a leather attaché case Suzanne hadn't seen before. Leith quickly apprised Tom of the situation, and Tom expressed his pleasure to both of them before Rolf pressed a glass of champagne into his hand and insisted he sit down and relax.

"What have you been up to, Tom?" Rolf asked the moment he was settled.

"I was solving a problem." His dark eyes swept slowly and consideringly around all of them. "It's just as well all four of you are here. It will save telling the story again and again."

"What story?" Leith asked.

"I have a good memory for some things." His gaze moved to Suzanne. "To see is to remember. You know that's how it is for me, Suzanne."

"I've never known you to be wrong, Tom," she agreed, the gravity of his words and expression urging her to confirm the accuracy of his visual memory. It was as though he carried imprints in his mind, particularly of people and places.

He turned his attention to Madeleine. "Last night you showed me photographs of your lost daughter. Would you be so kind as to bring that album here now, Mrs. Carew? I do not think I have made a mistake, but to be absolutely certain..."

Rolf leaned forward restively. "What are you getting at, Tom? What's Madeleine's daughter got to do with this problem you've been solving?"

"I believe I have found your wife's lost daughter, Mr. Carew," Tom stated quietly.

This was no little stone, Suzanne thought. It was like dropping a massive boulder into a pond. Ripples of tension swirled around the room, making everyone stiffen as different emotions gripped each person. There were several moments of shocked silence, during which Suzanne began to doubt that what Tom had said was possible. Then Rolf erupted from the sofa, his voice shaking with the threat of violence.

"If this is some damnable trick to get the reward..."

Leith sprang to his feet. "Hold it right there, Dad!" he commanded, raising a warding-off arm. "I know for a fact that Tom James has no personal interest in money."

"You know how many con men tried this on us?" his father raged. "Raising our hopes, tearing Madeleine's heart out—"

"Tom did not take the reward for Amy!" Leith cut in fiercely. "He's a man of the utmost integrity. He may be mistaken but he's not playing a heartless trick."

"You think it's credible after all these years?" his father jeered. "You think—"

"Rolf, please." Madeleine was suddenly beside him, pressing a restraining hand on his arm, her beautiful face white with strain but her eyes eloquently begging his forbearance. "If there's a chance..."

Rolf's face twisted with anguish. "I won't have you go through this again, Madeleine. Not again."

"Rolf, I know it cost you Ilana's love and Leith's. I can never make up for that. I can't bring Ilana back, and Leith—'' she gave her stepson a look that begged forgiveness ''—your happiness doesn't depend on anything we do now, does it, Leith?''

He shook his head.

"Madeleine." Rolf covered her hand, squeezing it in his turbulent emotion. "We have Jeb and Stuart. Are we to sacrifice them, as well, in pursuing what in all probability will be another dead end?"

"No, Mr. Carew," Tom interposed with quiet authority. "This will be settled tonight. Here and now. If Mrs. Carew will bring me her photograph album, I give you my word there will be no ongoing problem."

Rolf made a sound of bitter disbelief.

Suzanne could not hold silent. "Mr. Carew, please give my brother the opportunity to prove what he says."

As he turned to her, she stood and curled her arm around Leith's, reminding them all that she would soon be part of their family. She met the blazing mistrust in Rolf's eyes with calm steadiness. Although she sent up a silent prayer that Tom had not made some dreadful mistake, there was no question that she had to give him her loyalty and support.

"I know you don't know me very well, Mr. Carew. Nor Tom. But everyone adopted into our family, all fourteen of us, were lost children. We know what that means, better than most other people in the world. Tom would not say what he has said lightly. Not unless he was certain in his own mind. I ask you to give him your trust."

"So do I," Leith supported her without hesitation.

Rolf eyed his son in pained confusion. "You hated me for doing what you now urge me to."

"I didn't understand," Leith said gruffly, giving Suzanne a look that said he would walk to the end of the earth for her. "Now I do."

Rolf heaved a deep sigh and turned to his wife. "Please don't count on it too much, Madeleine. Remember what we have now?" he pleaded.

She reached up to give him a loving kiss. "I promise it won't hurt us, Rolf. Or the twins."

His arms went around her, hugging her tightly to him before slowly releasing her, a struggle of fear and love on his face. "One last time," he conceded grimly.

"Thank you, Rolf." She slid away from him and walked to a beautiful antique secretaire that graced one corner of the room. From a drawer she lifted out the photograph album that Tom had requested. That it was one of her most precious possessions was evident in the way she carried it to Tom and presented it to him.

Tom slowly leafed through it, only glancing at the photographs until he came to the one that had struck some chord of recognition in him last night.

"This is your daughter, Mrs. Carew?" he asked, pointing it out to her.

"Yes. As you can see, that photograph was taken on her birthday," Madeleine confirmed.

Tom nodded, then carefully placed the album on the coffee table next to the sofa where he sat. "When I saw it last night, I thought I had seen it before. I could not remember where. But then my dream came back to me—"

"Tom," Suzanne broke in urgently, afraid the others wouldn't understand about Tom's dreaming and be put off by it. Her eyes flashed a hard warning at him. "I don't think Mr. and Mrs. Carew want to hear about your dreams. However interesting they may be."

A rueful look flitted over his dark face. "Well, I remembered where it was. So today I went to Adelaide, then flew to Sydney to get the evidence so that I could show you."

"What evidence?" Rolf demanded curtly.

Tom picked up the attaché case he had brought in with him, set it on his knees, opened it and drew out a photograph, which he handed to Madeleine. "Wouldn't you say this photograph is identical in every way to the one in your album?"

Rolf moved to her side to look, as well.

Madeleine's hand began to tremble as she stared at it. "Where did you get this, Tom?" she asked huskily.

"It's a copy, Madeleine," Rolf said hastily. "It doesn't mean anything. It could have been picked up anywhere. It could have been copied from the one you have in your album."

"No. No." She shook her head in agitated denial. "Look how old it is, Rolf. And I sent him a copy. I always did. It only seemed fair at the time."

"Madeleine, you're making too much of this," Rolf protested, intensely disturbed by his wife's leap to a conclusion he couldn't or wouldn't accept. "Old photographs can be mislaid anywhere. Negatives left around and developed by someone else. It's not a lead to anything definite."

She swallowed convulsively. "Where did you get it from, Tom?"

"If you turn the photograph over, Mrs. Carew, there is handwriting on the back. Perhaps you will recognise it," Tom suggested softly.

Rolf snatched it from her hand and turned it over. Madeleine clutched his arm as they both stared at whatever was written. "It's *his* handwriting, Rolf," she cried. "And the words. He'd made up his mind to take her even then."

"This could all be a trick, Madeleine," Rolf warned, his voice harsh with concern. "Nothing but a clever forgery. We'd have to check with an expert." He swung a beetling look at Tom. "How did it come into your possession?" he demanded.

Madeleine, however, would not be shaken from what she wanted to believe. "Who is she now, Tom? Where is she? In Sydney?"

Tom did not give either of them a direct reply. Instead he said, "Would you please show the photograph to Suzanne?"

Suzanne frowned at him, reluctant to be drawn into such a personal issue between Rolf and Madeleine.

"You can confirm where the photograph came from," Tom pressed softly.

Rolf stepped over and thrust the photograph at her in an impatient gesture. She didn't take it. Her whole body froze as she stared at the picture of a little girl in a cowgirl suit standing beside a table where a cake with two candles alight was waiting for the child to blow the candles out.

She could feel the blood draining from her face as her heart stopped pumping. Her lungs forgot their function, as well. Black dots danced in front of her eyes. Her mind spun in circles like the ripples from a stone thrown into a pond, spilling down a river, sweeping into a wide estuary and far beyond, crossing oceans to the other side of the world, to Calgary, in Canada, where her father had died in a ring event, and a photograph was taken from his wallet, the only personal possession that linked the dead man to the little girl who had been found by Zachary Lee James and taken under the warm secure wing of his adopted parents.

Rolf did not have to turn the photograph over. Suzanne knew what was written on the back. "My little girl. For keeps," she whispered, then felt herself falling as her body gave up and let her slide into oblivion.

CHAPTER SIXTEEN

SUZANNE SLOWLY became aware of something wet and cool stroking her forehead. She heard Tom's voice as though from a far distance, recounting what had happened all those years ago in Calgary.

Then Madeleine's voice. "My first husband was a rancher." She spoke the words stiffly, as though finding it difficult to move her vocal cords. "But he sold up before...before—" A choking sound. "His favourite song was 'Oh, Susannah.'"

A memory floated through Suzanne's mind. She could see her father at the driving wheel of a truck, grinning at her as they sang the song together. They always sang it when travelling from one place to another.

Madeleine's voice intruded again, its deep distress penetrating the haze in Suzanne's mind. "I always thought I'd recognise her. But I didn't. I should have felt it. But I didn't. I should have..."

"Well, there can be no doubting it, Madeleine," Rolf said gruffly. "She is your daughter."

"Oh, Rolf! I knew she was special when she came into Amy's bedroom that first morning. But

it didn't enter my mind, not the slightest ink-
ling—"

"Madeleine!" Leith's voice cut in. "Don't make
Suzanne feel bad because your dream of recognising her didn't come true."

"It's too much for her to take in, Leith," Rolf
defended his wife. "Think what it feels like for
Madeleine to have had her daughter in her own
home for days and not to know it. And but for Tom
James, she would never have known it."

"She knows it now," Leith said definitively.
"And I don't want her upsetting Suzanne with the
idea they should have recognised each other. The
least you can do is consider her feelings first."

No, it's more complex than that, Suzanne
thought, struggling to draw enough strength to face
what had happened. There were so many feelings to
consider. *Coils within coils.*

"I brought one of our family albums with me so
that you can see Suzanne at every age, Mrs.
Carew," Tom quietly interposed.

"Thank you," Madeleine whispered. "How can
I thank you? After all these years . . ."

Twenty-two years. And if Ilana and Hans hadn't
died in the desert . . . Suzanne stirred at that dis-
quieting thought. Yet Tom would say nothing happened without a purpose, that life and death were
part of a continuous flow. But why did there have
to be so much pain along the way? For everyone.

"She's coming around," Leith announced with deep relief. "Everything's all right, Suzanne," he added soothingly. "You've come home. That's all that's happened. Home to all of us."

It was a wet cloth being gently applied to her face. Her eyelids felt sluggish, but Suzanne managed to lift them. She was lying on the sofa, her head and shoulders propped up by cushions. Leith was sitting near her waist, his face hovering anxiously over hers.

"You fainted," he said softly.

Suzanne had never fainted in her life before but she knew shock could do that to people. Somehow it was difficult to form words. She heard them slur from her lips. "Sorry. Made a fool of myself."

"Not at all!" Rolf's voice insisted. "Perfectly natural reaction."

Her gaze slowly lifted to find him but struck Madeleine first. She was standing behind Leith's shoulder, her lustrous dark eyes staring intensely at Suzanne, perhaps searching for the likeness to the child she had lost, the child Tom had found for her.

And Suzanne stared at the mother she hadn't been able to remember, the mother who hadn't died or abandoned her child, the mother who had searched and grieved all these years for the beloved daughter who had been stolen from her.

"Maria?" The name whispered from Madeleine's lips.

It puckered Suzanne's brow as it flowed through her mind, trying to find an echo. There was none. She had been Suzanne as far back as she could remember.

"Don't lay any more stress on her, Madeleine," Leith quickly advised. "Tom shouldn't have done it this way."

"It was the best way. Suzanne will understand," Tom said with quiet confidence.

Her eyes flicked to Rolf, standing beside Madeleine, concern and regret etched on his face. Concern for the stepdaughter he had not known, regret for his doubts that had led Tom into taking the course he had. Tom would not have expected her to faint from shock, but the reaction was so extreme, any suspicion of fakery had been convincingly wiped from Rolf's mind.

Suzanne understood, but where did they go from here? It complicated everything. Leith didn't like Madeleine. However much Suzanne might feel drawn to her, a mother she had never known was not as important to her as the man she loved. Her eyes returned anxiously to Leith's. How did he feel about this?

"It's all right, Suzanne," he soothed again. "You don't have to do anything you don't want to."

"No, you don't," Madeleine affirmed in a surprisingly strong voice. It drew their attention to her. She looked at Leith, her eyes steady with resolution. "I know you see me as obsessive and possessive. But you're wrong, Leith. I do not want to come between you and Suzanne in any way. What you have together... I would never want to hurt that."

Her eyes moved to Suzanne, softening with understanding of her apprehensions. "It's enough for me to know you're alive. And well. And very happy with a man you love. I could not wish more for my daughter. And I'm so proud of the person you've become. The beautiful woman you are. You're all I ever dreamed for my daughter to be. I am content with that, Suzanne."

"And I've never been prouder of you, my love," Rolf said huskily, sliding his arm around his wife's shoulders and hugging her close to him.

"Suzanne?" Leith called her attention to him.

"There's been so much hurt, Leith," she said, searching his eyes for a response to Madeleine's generous sacrifice of all self-interest for the sake of their happiness.

"Too much," he agreed. "I've misread the situation very badly, not understanding all it involved. And if I'd never met you, I never would have understood, Suzanne. Loving you..."

"You can still love me, Leith?" she broke in. "Even though you now know it was me they were looking for? And despite how badly that hurt you and Ilana?"

His arms instantly burrowed beneath her and lifted her into a fierce embrace. "Always. Forever," he said passionately. "How you can still think of others when you've suffered so much yourself..." A long, shuddering sigh wavered through her hair. "I love you, Suzanne. Nothing will ever change that."

Relief surged through her, easing her most urgent concerns. "I love you, too," she murmured for the sheer bliss of saying it. Then with more confidence, she asked, "Do you think we can lay the past to rest now, Leith?"

He drew back enough to smile at her, his eyes caressing her soul with all he felt for her. "You make anything possible, Suzanne."

"I really think your father loves you," she tried, hoping Leith would accept it.

He swept his smile to Rolf and Madeleine, then returned sparkling eyes to Suzanne. "And I'm completely convinced your mother loves you."

Unclouded joy zinged through her heart. "Then let's celebrate again," she said eagerly, turning her smile to the two people who had been awaiting their decision. "With my new family. And my old one."

Her gaze moved lovingly to her brother, standing slightly apart, watching with that look of age-old wisdom in his eyes. "Thank you, Tom."

LEITH AND SUZANNE decided not to hurry their marriage plans. Leith insisted it was only fair that she and Madeleine have some time together after all the years of separation, so they agreed that three months wasn't too long to wait. It wasn't as though they had to be apart. The Barossa Valley was close enough to Adelaide for Leith to commute to work each day.

Amy blossomed under all the loving attention everyone gave her. Jeb and Stuart were fascinated to find out that Suzanne was their half-sister and quickly decided that their older half-brother had definitely got it right in choosing her as his wife-to-be. Their respect for Leith's judgment moved up several notches. They gave him credit for bringing her home, although Tom did take the laurels for identifying her.

The empathy Suzanne had felt with her natural mother strengthened with every day that passed. Learning about each other's lives gave a sense of fulfilment to all the wondering both of them had done. Initially Madeleine was careful not to press for any show of affection, but Suzanne was happy to give her the assurance that gestures of affection were not unwelcome.

The relationship between Leith and his father lost all tension and became warmly genial. The house took on a relaxed, happy atmosphere that Gertrude remarked on with great satisfaction. "It was good that you came here," she told Suzanne with beaming approval. "Now everyone eats well.

Nothing bad to take away the appetite. Everything good!''

And so it felt to Suzanne. Privately she put it down to a peace of mind that none of them had had before, not herself or Leith or Rolf or Madeleine. Or perhaps it was peace of heart. There was no longer anything missing from their lives. The sense of completeness gave them the freedom to be happy.

Everything felt more complete on Suzanne's and Leith's wedding day. They had decided on a ceremony in the beautiful grounds of the Carew home, and the weather could not have been more benevolent, with clear blue skies and bright sunlight making the gardens and lawns vivid with colour.

All the James family had come to meet Suzanne's new family and wish her every happiness in her marriage to Leith. Suzanne's adopted mother, as giving in her loving as she always was, insisted that Madeleine take over all the duties of being mother of the bride. So it was Madeleine who helped Suzanne into her wedding finery and shed emotional tears when there was no more to do and her daughter stood before her with that special beauty a bride always has.

''This means so much to me,'' she said huskily. ''Every mother dreams of her daughter's wedding. I thought it could only ever be a dream for me. To see you like this, to be with you...''

"I know," Suzanne said softly. She took her mother's hand and lifted it to her cheek, leaning into its warm palm as her eyes shone their love at the woman who had given birth to her. "Thank you for wanting me. For answering all the questions that haunted my dreams. For being all I could wish my mother to be. You make this day very special for me, too."

Madeleine took a deep breath then smiled through her tears, a brilliant smile that sparkled with deep inner joy. "I mustn't keep you from Leith. It's time."

"Yes," Suzanne agreed, her heart swelling with happiness as she thought of the man waiting for her, the man whose love had given her a new life.

Her adopted father took her arm to walk her down the temporarily constructed aisle. She had a fleeting thought of her natural father, hoping his spirit was at peace, as well. Then the music started and everyone turned to smile at her.

Amy led the way in her role as flower girl, happily scattering rose petals on the lawn from a much beribboned basket. Suzanne couldn't help thinking how very multinational her adopted family looked today, each one of them so individual in their choice of dress.

There was a slight pause in the wedding march when Amy forgot what she was supposed to be doing and stared up at Suzanne's American brother, Zachary Lee. He was a big bear of a man, well over six feet, with massive shoulders and a huge barrel chest. His rich chestnut hair framed a face that invited trust. Some innate quality in him invariably drew children like a magnet. He leaned down, and in his gentle, kindly fashion, reminded Amy to get on with her job.

A knowing grin spread around the rest of the family. It was always like that with Zachary Lee. He was *the* big brother to all of them, and when he turned his smile to Suzanne, she thanked whatever providence had led her to him when she was lost.

But she wasn't lost any more, and never would be again with Leith beside her. Her gaze turned to the man she loved above all others, and the sheer adoration in his eyes made her heart catch. When he held out his hand to her and she placed her palm on his, the feeling of oneness with him was absolute.

The ceremony was simple but intensely moving for Suzanne and Leith as they pledged their love to each other in words that expressed the deep commitment in their hearts and souls. When her Chinese brother, Zuang Chi, lifted his magnificent voice to sing Beethoven's beautiful "Song of Joy," Suzanne felt as though angels were singing inside her, and the look in Leith's eyes told her he felt it, too. Today was their day in the sun, the beginning of their life as husband and wife.

As they turned together to receive the well wishes of their families, Suzanne caught Tom's eyes, and they smiled at each other, a private, intimate smile.

In her mind she could hear him saying what she now knew to be true.

For Leith Carew, you are his passion. There is no mistaking the shining of that kind of love.

And that was what Leith and she would always hold within them . . . the shining of love.

A Last Word

In recent times, the adoption laws in Australia have been altered so that if both parties are willing, and in strictly controlled circumstances, adopted children can seek out their natural parents, and vice versa. Many stories have come to light of strange, almost incredible cross lines in the lives of both the adopted children and the natural parents, with neither party knowing or recognising any relationship to the other. Similarities in character, ambitions, careers, mannerisms or physical features did not raise any questions in these people's minds. Not until the truth was known did the range of coincidences take on any meaning. Should any reader think this story improbable, the author can only say it was inspired by true stories... and truth is far stranger than fiction.

POSTCARDS FROM EUROPE

HARLEQUIN PRESENTS®

Travel across Europe in 1994 with Harlequin Presents. Collect a new *Postcards From Europe* title each month!

Don't miss
DARK SUNLIGHT
by Patricia Wilson
Harlequin Presents #1644

Available in April, wherever Harlequin Presents books are sold.

HPPFE4

Hi—

The sun was shining brightly here in Spain *until* I met Felipe de Santis. The man is used to giving orders and doesn't respect my abilities as a journalist. But I'm going to get my story—and I'm going to help Felipe's sister!

Love, Maggie

P.S. If only I could win Felipe's love....

Take 4 bestselling love stories FREE

Plus get a FREE surprise gift!

Special Limited-time Offer

Mail to Harlequin Reader Service®

P. O. Box 609
Fort Erie, Ontario
L2A 5X3

YES! Please send me 4 free Harlequin Presents® novels and my free surprise gift. Then send me 6 brand-new novels every month, which I will receive months before they appear in bookstores. Bill me at the low price of $2.49 each—plus 25¢ delivery and GST *. That's the complete price and compared to the cover prices of $2.99 each—quite a bargain! I understand that accepting the books and gift places me under no obligation ever to buy any books. I can always return a shipment and cancel at any time. Even if I never buy another book from Harlequin, the 4 free books and the surprise gift are mine to keep forever.

306 BPA AJT

Name _____ (PLEASE PRINT)

Address _____ Apt. No. _____

City _____ Province _____ Postal Code _____

This offer is limited to one order per household and not valid to present Harlequin Presents® subscribers. *Terms and prices are subject to change without notice. Canadian residents will be charged applicable provincial taxes and GST.

CPRES-94R   ©1990 Harlequin Enterprises Limited

When the only time you have for yourself is...

Spring into spring—by giving yourself a March Break! Take a few *stolen moments* and treat yourself to a Great Escape. Relax with one of our brand-new stories (or with all six!).

Each STOLEN MOMENTS title in our Great Escapes collection is a complete and never-before-published *short* novel. These contemporary romances are 96 pages long—the perfect length for the busy woman of the nineties!

Look for Great Escapes in our Stolen Moments display this March!

SIZZLE by Jennifer Crusie
ANNIVERSARY WALTZ
by Anne Marie Duquette
MAGGIE AND HER COLONEL
by Merline Lovelace
PRAIRIE SUMMER by Alina Roberts
THE SUGAR CUP by Annie Sims
LOVE ME NOT by Barbara Stewart

Wherever Harlequin and Silhouette books are sold.

SMGE

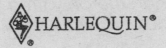

HARLEQUIN®

MARRIAGE *BY Design*

Harlequin proudly presents four stories about
convenient but not *conventional* reasons for marriage:

- ◆ To save your godchildren from a
  "wicked stepmother"

- ◆ To help out your eccentric aunt—and her sexy
  business partner

- ◆ To bring an old man happiness by making him
  a grandfather

- ◆ To escape from a ghostly existence and become a
  real woman

Marriage By Design—four brand-new stories by four
of Harlequin's most popular authors:

**CATHY GILLEN THACKER
JASMINE CRESSWELL
GLENDA SANDERS
MARGARET CHITTENDEN**

Don't miss this exciting collection of stories about
marriages of convenience. Available in April, wherever
Harlequin books are sold.

Fifty red-blooded, white-hot, true-blue hunks
from every State in the Union!

Look for MEN MADE IN AMERICA! Written by some of
our most popular authors, these stories feature fifty of
the strongest, sexiest men, each from a different state in
the union!

Two titles available every other month at your favorite
retail outlet.

In March, look for:

TANGLED LIES by Anne Stuart (Hawaii)
ROGUE'S VALLEY by Kathleen Creighton (Idaho)

In April, look for:

LOVE BY PROXY by Diana Palmer (Illinois)
POSSIBLES by Lass Small (Indiana)

You won't be able to resist MEN MADE IN AMERICA!

HARLEQUIN®

Don't miss these Harlequin favorites by some of our most distinguished authors!
And now, you can receive a discount by ordering two or more titles!

HT#25409	THE NIGHT IN SHINING ARMOR by JoAnn Ross	$2.99 ☐
HT#25471	LOVESTORM by JoAnn Ross	$2.99 ☐
HP#11463	THE WEDDING by Emma Darcy	$2.89 ☐
HP#11592	THE LAST GRAND PASSION by Emma Darcy	$2.99 ☐
HR#03188	DOUBLY DELICIOUS by Emma Goldrick	$2.89 ☐
HR#03248	SAFE IN MY HEART by Leigh Michaels	$2.89 ☐
HS#70464	CHILDREN OF THE HEART by Sally Garrett	$3.25 ☐
HS#70524	STRING OF MIRACLES by Sally Garrett	$3.39 ☐
HS#70500	THE SILENCE OF MIDNIGHT by Karen Young	$3.39 ☐
HI#22178	SCHOOL FOR SPIES by Vickie York	$2.79 ☐
HI#22212	DANGEROUS VINTAGE by Laura Pender	$2.89 ☐
HI#22219	TORCH JOB by Patricia Rosemoor	$2.89 ☐
HAR#16459	MACKENZIE'S BABY by Anne McAllister	$3.39 ☐
HAR#16466	A COWBOY FOR CHRISTMAS by Anne McAllister	$3.39 ☐
HAR#16462	THE PIRATE AND HIS LADY by Margaret St. George	$3.39 ☐
HAR#16477	THE LAST REAL MAN by Rebecca Flanders	$3.39 ☐
HH#28704	A CORNER OF HEAVEN by Theresa Michaels	$3.99 ☐
HH#28707	LIGHT ON THE MOUNTAIN by Maura Seger	$3.99 ☐

Harlequin Promotional Titles

#83247	YESTERDAY COMES TOMORROW by Rebecca Flanders	$4.99 ☐
#83257	MY VALENTINE 1998	$4.99 ☐
	(short-story collection featuring Anne Stuart, Judith Arnold, Anne McAllister, Linda Randall Wisdom)	

(limited quantities available on certain titles)

	AMOUNT	$
DEDUCT:	10% DISCOUNT FOR 2+ BOOKS	$
ADD:	POSTAGE & HANDLING	$
	($1.00 for one book, 50¢ for each additional)	
	APPLICABLE TAXES*	$ _____
	TOTAL PAYABLE	$ _____
	(check or money order—please do not send cash)	

To order, complete this form and send it, along with a check or money order for the total above, payable to Harlequin Books, to: **In the U.S.:** 3010 Walden Avenue, P.O. Box 9047, Buffalo, NY 14269-9047; **In Canada:** P.O. Box 613, Fort Erie, Ontario, L2A 5X3.

Name: _____

Address: _____ City: _____

State/Prov.: _____ Zip/Postal Code: _____

*New York residents remit applicable sales taxes.
  Canadian residents remit applicable GST and provincial taxes.

HBACK-JM